'Now follow me!' ... noise of stamping ...

He broke throu... ... the way round th... ...headquarters, fol-
lowed by the line of puffing youngsters. But Akela did not return to the lawn behind the Cub headquarters. He ran out through the gate, over the stone bridge and along the path which meandered alongside the little stream through the woods.

'Where's he going? Where's he going?' gasped Nobby, chugging along behind Snowy. 'Where's he gone?'

'Looks like he's taking us for a cross-country run,' Snowy blurted out.

'Cross which country?' gasped Nobby.

Also in Beaver by Stephen Andrews

Cubs with a Difference

CUBS AWAY

Stephen Andrews

Illustrated by Val Biro

Beaver Books

A Beaver Book

Published by Arrow Books Limited
17-21 Conway Street, London W1P 6JD

A division of the Hutchinson Publishing Group

London Melbourne Sydney Auckland
Johannesburg and agencies throughout
the world

First published
by Hodder and Stoughton 1974
Beaver edition 1985

Printed and bound in Great Britain by
Anchor Brendon Limited, Tiptree, Essex

ISBN 0 09 938100 1

Contents

1 · Out and about

AKELA gathered the 2nd Billington Cub Scout Pack in a large circle around him, on the lawn behind the red-bricked Cub headquarters. He waited for complete silence.

Christopher Clark, or 'Nobby' as this clown prince of Cubs was known, put his hand over his eyes and mumbled to himself.

'I promise to help God and the Queen to do a good turn every day, and to help myself at all times . . .'

'Ssh!' said Georgie White, his Sixer, who was better known as 'Snowy'. Snowy stood as erect as a guardsman, with the peak of his cap over his eyes. He spoke out of the side of his mouth. 'Akela is waiting.'

Nobby groaned. 'It's all right for you, Snowy. You are brainy, you know the Cub Scout Promise and Law. I don't! Akela said he's going to see if I know and understand them tonight, but a fat chance I have of showing him, I must say. I suppose I know them well enough, or the idea behind them, until I have to say

them, then I get them all mixed up. If I were the
Chief Scout, the first thing I'd do would be to change
all those wordy words to something simple such as
"God save the Queen, I hope I've been, the best
Cub you've seen, 'cos I'm very keen", and leave it at
that.'

'I'll run through them with you before you see
Akela,' said Snowy. 'You know them, you'll have no
trouble repeating them if you don't panic and get
yourself mixed up.'

'I don't know about that,' grunted Nobby.

Of course, Nobby had shown Akela that he had
really known and understood the Promise and Law
soon after he had joined the Cubs. How he had
managed to do that, no one could say, for Nobby had
not appeared to have understood anything either
before or since.

How he should have recited the Promise and Law in
the first place is still a mystery, but Nobby had
recognized his weakness – he is the first to admit he is
a bonehead – and he did what he could to make up for
his deficiency. He had written, in indelible ink, the
Cub Scout Promise on his right palm, and the Cub
Scout Law on his left, and he could recite them reasonably well by alternately putting his hands on his
eyebrows, in the pose of a great thinker.

Akela had asked Nobby to tell him the Cub Scout

Promise and Law with his hands by his sides, but it was like asking a donkey to recite Shakespeare. Nobby insisted that he must be allowed to adopt the pose of a great thinker. Akela agreed, provided Nobby wore a pair of boxing-gloves, and miracle upon miracle, Nobby said his lines. Akela raised the boy's arm, as if he had just won a boxing match. Nobby waved to his pals, as if he was the new heavyweight champion. He was a parrot in boxing gloves, but he had earned himself his first badge – the Cub Scout Badge – and so became a real Cub Scout and a member of the world wide brotherhood of Scouts. He was able to wear this 'World Badge', so called because many people in Scouting in countries all over the world wear this same badge. Nobby was going to wear it. It shows that Scouts, young or old, small or very important, whatever language they speak, are all just Scouts. Nobby was proud of the badge he had earned. Happy Scouting! Two days later he was as hopeless as ever.

As it was Akela's intention to make sure his Cubs properly understood their Promise and Law, he periodically asked the Cubs about them. He was a sportsman though, for he had given Nobby plenty of warning that it was almost his turn to be checked again, and Akela told his Pack plenty of stories of Scouts who had used the Promise and Law to benefit others. Nobby, in his enthusiasm, had prepared himself by writing the Promise and Law on his wrists, knees, dirty handkerchief and shirt tail.

Outside the Cub headquarters, on that fine summer evening, Akela glowered at Nobby. Nobby scratched his nose, then stood reasonably still. At last Akela had the full attention of his Cubs. He looked up into the cloudless, blue sky and took a deep breath of the cool, fresh air.

'As it is such a beautiful evening,' he said, lightly, 'I have decided to change our planned programme. I won't be telling you any stories or going through your badge requirements.'

The Cubs cheered. Nobby heaved a sigh of relief.

'Don't you like my stories?' asked Akela, somewhat hurt. Akela always gave very interesting talks on badge subjects which the Cubs enjoyed, but on this particular fine evening, there was not one Cub who was enthusiastic about staying indoors.

'We'd prefer to do some real outdoor Scouting on a night like this,' said Snowy, 'if you don't mind.'

'Oh?' said Akela. He looked around until his eyes rested on Nobby. 'Don't you want to tell us your Law and Promise, Nobby?'

'Yes . . . yes . . . yes . . .,' blabbered Nobby, 'yes . . . yes . . . but next Friday will be soon enough for me.'

Akela smiled. 'You are right. Indoor subjects should take second place in the Cubs. There are many other activities which we should not neglect, especially when the weather is as beautiful as it is now. There'll be plenty of other times for you to earn yourselves badges, times when it is cold and wet, but tonight we'll turn our minds to other things. Now Cubs, I want you to do what I do.'

Akela slowly raised his arms. The Cubs did likewise.

'I did not ask you to hold hands,' said Akela to two Cubs who happened to be standing close to one another. 'I am not going to ask you to play "ring-a-ring of roses" or to "come dancing". Now do this.'

Akela put his feet astride. The Cubs did likewise. Next, Akela bent right down and put his right hand on his left toe. He raised himself then he put his left hand on his right toe. Little bones creaked around the great circle. The Cubs wheezed and groaned.

'You are like a lot of old codgers,' said Akela. 'Your joints need oiling. Now do this.'

Akela began jogging on the spot. The Cubs joined in, and taking their timing from their Cub Scout Leader, their legs moved faster, and faster, and faster, until they were going like little steam engines.

'Now follow me!' shouted Akela above the noise of stamping feet.

He broke through the ring of Cubs and led the way round the Cub headquarters, followed by the line of

puffing youngsters. But Akela did not return to the
lawn behind the Cub headquarters. He ran out through
the gate, over the stone bridge and along the path
which meandered alongside the little stream through
the woods.

'Where's he going? Where's he going?' gasped
Nobby, chugging along behind Snowy. 'Where's he
gone?'

'Looks like he's taking us for a cross-country run,'
Snowy blurted out.

'Cross which country?' gasped Nobby. 'He might
have told us. My stomach is still back at H Q.'

But the Cubs had little time to collect their

thoughts. From the start, Akela set a cracking pace, and such was the spirit of the 2nd Billingtons, that every single Cub was determined to give his best and not let his Six down.

All would have been well had not the Cubs happened to pass an old gentleman coming the other way, taking his dog for a walk. The dog was a large, stupid Great Dane, which for some strange reason immediately took a liking to Nobby. It bounded along after Nobby in spite of the calls of its owner to come back.

'Clarence, Clarence,' called the old gentleman. 'You're going the wrong way. Come back, Clarence.'

But Clarence bounded on after Nobby who, yelling out in terror, ran as fast as his flat feet would carry him. Snowy tried to catch Clarence, but it didn't want to know him. All it wanted, apparently, was Nobby

'Jump across the stream! Jump across the stream!' suggested Snowy.

'In the stream?' said Nobby.

'Over the stream,' said Snowy.

'Good idea,' gasped Nobby.

Nobby ran on, not stopping, but keeping his eyes open for a suitable narrow part of the stream to leap across. He found what he was looking for at a bend. He sprinted ahead, and leapt over it. Nobby slithered on the far bank and fell flat on his face, but he had made it.

However, the Great Dane was not to be put off. It waddled through the muddy stream, poked Nobby with a muddy paw, and when Nobby rolled over, it licked his cheek.

'Get off!' said Nobby, trying to get away. 'Don't wipe your dirty feet on me, you great nelephant.'

Nobby leapt back across the stream, the Great Dane waddled after him and Snowy caught it by the collar. The beast was tremendously strong, but with Nobby helping, by letting it nuzzle him, Snowy managed to hold it until the old gentleman caught up with them.

'Clarence, you naughty thing,' said the old gentleman, clipping on its leash. 'You'll be back in the doghouse when I get you home. You're up to your ears in mud!'

'He's not the only one,' grunted Nobby.

The old gentleman walked away, dragging his reluctant hound with him. The Cubs were left in peace, but the event had left them at least three minutes behind the other Cubs in the cross-country run. Nobby brushed the paw-marks off his jersey.

'We'll have to hurry to catch up with the others,' said Snowy, anxiously. 'If we don't, we'll lose them.'

Nobby wiped his face with a dirty handkerchief. 'Hurry? Hurry? What do you think I've been doing but hurrying with that monster after me? Come on!'

The two Cubs ran off to catch up with their pals. They ran through the park gates and almost caught up with the last Cubs, whom they recognized by their red and green scarves.

Snowy slowed down, momentarily confused, for not only could he see he was following the Cubs of his own Pack, but, by a number of black and yellow scarves farther ahead, the Cubs from the 1st West Park Cub Scout Pack. Snowy carried on, to catch up with the stragglers, but again he stopped, for he was surprised when they turned off at the right fork in the park. The right fork, he knew led to a stone bridge and thence to the west side of the park. It was not usual for Akela to bring them so far.

As Snowy tried to fathom out this problem, he saw, to his surprise, Akela returning via the left fork, followed by some of his Cubs, in this case all 2nd Billingtons in their red and green scarves.

'Hurry up, straggler,' shouted Akela as he passed Snowy. 'Once round the fountain, and no cheating.'

Before Snowy could reply, Akela had jogged on, followed by about a dozen of his jogging Cubs.

'Come back, come back, wait a minute,' yelled Snowy, but they ran on, taking not the slightest notice of him.

Now half of the Cubs were returning to the Cub headquarters, but the others were going in the opposite direction, to West Park! Snowy ran up a near-by grassy hill. From there he could see, beyond the stream in the park valley, a column of Cubs struggling up the hill on the far side. Leading the field were the black and yellow scarved Cubs of West Park. In the middle were a couple of Cubs without scarves. Behind them were a dozen or so of red and green scarved Cubs of the 2nd Billingtons. Right at the back was Nobby, being chased by a couple of stray dogs.

Immediately Snowy realized what had happened. Because of the hot weather, the West Parkers too had decided to take a run in the park. Their stragglers had thrown off their choking scarves and had been mistaken by the 2nd Billingtons, for 2nd Billingtons. And now a dozen or so 2nd Billingtons, including Nobby and a couple of stray dogs, were being led to the West Park Cub headquarters.

Snowy dashed back down the slope to catch up with Akela. He knew Akela kept a very tight check on the Cubs under his control, and he would be extremely worried the moment he discovered any were missing. Snowy had to warn him before he called out the police and organized a full-scale search.

Snowy sprinted along the path beside the stream through the woods as fast as he could go. It was desperately hot. He clawed his red and green scarf

from his throat and stuffed it down his trouser top.
He realized why the West Park stragglers he had seen
without scarves had done likewise. Snowy ran on, in a
daze, but Akela had maintained his cracking pace and
Snowy did not catch up with him until he was back
at the Cub headquarters. Akela was waiting at the
gate, counting the Cubs as they came through.

'Where are the others, where are the others?' said
Akela, anxiously, as he saw no one behind Snowy.

Snowy collapsed on his haunches and tried to get
back his breath.

'They . . . they . . . they've gone to the 1st West
Park Cub headquarters,' gasped Snowy.

'West Park?' echoed Akela. 'What are they doing
there? What have the West Parkers got that the 2nd
Billingtons haven't? Hey, they haven't kidnapped
our lads, have they?'

'No, no, no,' explained Snowy. 'Some of ours got
mixed up with some of them and they all went off to
the West Park Cub headquarters.'

'Why, why, why, this is unbelievable!' gasped
Akela. 'Unbelievable! I bet Nobby's at the bottom of
this. We'll . . . we'll . . . we'll be the laughing-stock of
the whole Scout Movement. I'll . . . I'll hang the little
blighter from the flagpole.'

'Nobby had nothing to do with it,' said Snowy.

But Akela wasn't listening. 'Don't any of you move

outside the gates until I get back from the telephone,'
he said. 'Fine fool I'll look when I ring up the West
Park Cub Scout Leader. Have you got any of my Cubs
mixed up with your lot? He'll think I'm a raving
lunatic.'

Akela stormed off to the telephone kiosk just
outside the Cub headquarters, but when he returned
he was grinning all over his face.

'The laugh's on us, lads,' he said. 'Our lads are
having a whale of a time with the West Parkers.
We've been invited to join the party. Take your seats
in the Scout mini-bus. We'll drive over there in style
to join them.'

The mini-bus belonged to the Scout Group. Because
the Cubs had helped to raise money to buy it, by
doing jobs such as washing cars on Saturday mornings,
Akela was allowed to use it for his Cubs, every
Friday evening, or at week-ends when it was not
otherwise booked. It was an old airport bus, but the
Venture Scouts in particular had put in a lot of work
to keep it roadworthy. The Scouts had repainted it
red and green, the Group colours, and the Cubs had
helped where they could by cleaning it and polishing
up the chrome-work.

So what was left of the 2nd Billingtons drove the
long way round to the West Park Cub headquarters.
There they found their companions playing hand-

football with a West Park team. The host Cub Scout Leader blew his whistle to stop the game, and welcomed the newcomers warmly.

'It's with great pleasure that I welcome our friendly rivals from Billington,' he said. 'I always feel excited when I'm at a gathering of Cub Packs. It seems to bring out the Pack spirit. Of course, I haven't forgotten that the 2nd Billingtons took the Cheshire Cup from us last year, and if they think they are still top dogs this year, well, we are always ready to show them otherwise. Mind you, I don't for one moment want to suggest that our attitude towards the 2nd Billingtons is not one of friendship. We want to develop our ties of friendship with our neighbours. There is no room in the Scout Movement for . . . for . . .' The West Park Cub Scout Leader was stuck for a word. 'What's the opposite of friendship?'

There was a pause while the Cubs of both Packs searched their brains for the right word.

'Opposite of friendship?' said Nobby from the floor. 'Why, battleship!'

'Battleship?' echoed the Cub Scout Leader. 'There's no room for battleship! What am I talking about? Anyway, you know what I mean. The 1st West Park Pack is ready to challenge you to any game you suggest.'

'Tiddlywinks!' yelled Nobby.

'Tiddlywinks?' echoed the Cub Scout Leader.

'Yeah, tiddlywinks,' repeated Nobby. 'We can whack you at tiddlywinks any day of the week, any hour of the day, and any second of the minute.'

'No, you couldn't,' said a West Parker.

'Yes, we could. Bets!'

'We could whack you with one eye closed.'

'No, you couldn't!'

'Yes, we could!'

'Prove it, then.'

'Cubs! Cubs! Cubs!'

So it was decided to have a tiddlywink competition. Each Six took on an opposing Six. Six games were played. To cut a long story short, the result was a draw, three games to the West Parkers and three games to Billington. Then, to settle the result of the game, it was decided to play one more game, the Billington Sixers versus the West Park Sixers.

The West Park team was good. They got four tiddlywinks in the plastic cup. But the Billingtons were equally good, for they, too, got four tiddlywinks in the plastic cup, and they had one more turn to go, the last go of the match. It was all up to Snowy. His tiddlywink was about half a metre from the plastic cup. If he could get it in, the 2nd Billingtons would be the undisputed champions.

Snowy lined up to take his shot. The excitement

was intense. The Cubs from both Packs crowded in to see the result.

'Come on, Snowy,' yelled Nobby, as he was hemmed in by the Cubs pressing down on all sides. 'Up the Billingtons!'

Snowy tiddled just as Nobby yelled out. The wink shot up into Nobby's gaping mouth, and Nobby gulped and swallowed it. For one moment there was an awful silence.

'Sit in the cup and we've won the match,' shouted Spotty, a Billington Cub.

'Good idea!' burped Nobby.

Nobby sat on the plastic cup and broke it and the cardboard box holding it. Immediately there was an uproar, and the two Cub Scout Leaders had to pull the rival Cubs apart. No one was quite sure enough of the rules of tiddlywinks to know whether the result should be a draw or a Billington win, although there was plenty of argument about it. However, no decision was made because of Nobby's sudden peculiar appearance. He turned quite white and everyone thought he was about to be sick.

'He needs a dose of castor oil,' shouted someone.

'We've got no castor oil. What do you think this is, Stockport supermarket?'

'There's a can of engine oil in the cupboard. Give 'im a dose of that.'

At the reference to engine oil, Nobby turned quite green, so the West Park Cub Scout Leader, who worked in the local hospital in some capacity, took him outside.

Nobby soon returned, none the worse for wear, having had three glasses of water to wash down his tiddlywink.

The Cub Scout Leaders were reluctant to continue the rival games, so the evening ended in a more civilized manner with a singsong. The West Park

Cubs showed they too knew something of true Scout comradeship, for they mingled freely with the 2nd Billingtons, and did their best to make their visitors feel welcome. The West Park Seconds supplied the Billingtons each with a free bottle of lemonade and a chocolate biscuit. Even Nobby admitted the West Parkers were a good crowd.

'We don't get free pop in our Pack, 'cept on special occasions,' Nobby confided in a West Park Sixer.

'Neither do we,' replied the Sixer, patting Nobby on the shoulder, 'but this *is* a special occasion. It's great to have you with us.'

The West Park Cub Scout Leader worked his way through the chatting Cubs to Nobby.

'How do you feel now, young man?' he asked.

Nobby gulped down a mouthful of biscuit. 'Fine,' he said. 'Can we come again next week?'

The leader patted Nobby on the head. 'You're all right,' he said. 'We will meet again.'

The rival Packs parted company, the best of friends. Those who had come in the Scout mini-bus, plus Nobby, were to return in the Scout mini-bus. The rest of the Billington Cubs were instructed to make their way back to Cub headquarters by the path by the stream.

'Smart Pack!' commented Snowy, as they drove away.

'Good night out!' said Nobby.

Akela smiled and wound down his cab window. 'If this fine weather holds, we'll have a few more adventures away from base,' he said. 'How about that? It's ridiculous staying indoors in good weather.'

Nobby grinned like an elf.

'I'm afraid I won't be asking you to tell us your Promise and Law again, Nobby,' Akela went on. 'I've no doubt you know them well enough, but it does help if you refresh your memory from time to time.' Akela took another deep breath of the cool, fresh air. 'It might be weeks before we get back to indoor activities.'

Nobby rolled his eyes and rubbed his hands.

'Goody, goody, goody!' he said.

2 · The making of a champion

THE fine weather held. The hot, midday sun beat down as the 2nd Billington Cub Scout Pack lined up in the car-park outside the swimming-pool entrance.

'Now don't forget to take a shower before you go into the pool,' Akela reminded them, 'and don't forget to give your feet a good wash.'

But the Cubs were not listening to him. They looked beyond their Cub Scout Leader to where an untidy street urchin, about their own age, was pulling a rail out of the chestnut fence which surrounded the swimming-pool car-park. He dragged the stick along the ground, scattering the gravel in wide sweeping movements. He stopped when he came up to a shiny new motorcycle, then he hit the front tyre, mudguard and handlebar with his stick. Then, to everyone's amazement, he put his dirty rolled-up towel on the ground, took up his stick in both hands and began to whack the petrol tank of the motorcycle as hard as he could.

Akela looked over his shoulder. For a moment he was speechless. He crept up on the unsuspecting boy, trying desperately hard not to strangle him.

'What are you doing?' bellowed Akela like a bull.

The youth looked at him sullenly. 'Nothing,' he grunted.

'Nothing?' echoed Akela. 'You young idiot! Don't you know that if you cracked that petrol tank, and petrol dripped on the hot engine, the whole thing would explode in flames, and you with it?'

'What's it got to do with you?' growled the youth, pouting.

'Do with me? I pay enough in taxes to pay for the vandalism caused by the likes of you,' growled Akela. 'Where did you get that stick?'

The youth swung the rail away. 'From that fence'.

'Well put it back,' ordered Akela, sternly. 'Put it back. Put it back or I'll call the police.'

The youth slouched across the car-park and picked up the rail. He dragged it back through the gravel and dropped it in the hole. All the time Akela hovered over him like a vulture.

'Properly!' growled Akela, 'and that means straight, like the others, the way you found it.'

The youth straightened the rail in the ground.

'You step out of line just once more, and you'll be for it, me lad. I'll have the police on you like a ton of

bricks. Don't think I'm joking. I'm not standing any
nonsense from the likes of you!'

The lad sneered, but he had the common sense not
to goad Akela any further. He knew Akela meant
business. He slouched across the car-park, picked up
his dirty towel and ambled into the entrance of the
swimming-pool.

Akela returned to his Cubs, still pale with fury. 'As
I was saying,' he said, his voice still trembling with
rage, 'don't forget to give your feet a good wash. I
don't want any of your germs polluting the pool.
Now file inside, and no messing about.'

The Cubs filed inside, visibly shaken by Akela's

anger, a mood they never expected to see in him. Yet inside the changing-rooms, the atmosphere of the pool took over. In a trice they were undressed and in the grounds of the beautiful open-air swimming-pool. For many it was their first visit. They gazed in wonder at the blue waters, and the towering white diving-tower.

'Whew, isn't it high?' said Nobby, goggling at the six-metre board.

Snowy gasped too. It was twice as high as anything he'd been off.

Akela blew his whistle. 'Non-swimmers at the shallow end. You can only go in the deep end if you have your Swimmer Badge.'

Akela lined up his non-swimmers in the shallow end to show them the movements of the breast stroke. Every Cub, and especially Nobby, was keen to learn for not only would they be able to sample the pleasures of swimming, but also they knew Akela was preparing them first for their Silver Arrow, then for their Gold Arrow and Swimmer Badge. Being keen Cubs, they wanted as many Cub badges as they could win. Snowy was fortunate in having had weekly swimming lessons at school. He amused himself by swimming free-style back and forth across a width of the deep end.

After ten minutes' instruction, the Cubs were

allowed to practise by themselves, or play about in the shallow end. Snowy dived in to join Nobby.

'How's it going, Nob? Can you swim yet?'

Nobby pushed back his wet hair. 'I know how to move my hands and I know how to move my legs, but for the life of me, I can't move them all together.'

But Nobby's lack of co-ordination did not prevent him from enjoying himself. Ungainly as he was, he leapt about in the water like a frollicking dolphin, until he exhausted himself. He pulled himself out of the pool to dry himself in the hot sun. Snowy flopped down beside him. Watching them spitefully was the urchin they had seen in the car-park. He ambled across and 'accidentally' trod on Nobby's foot.

'Ow!' yelled Nobby, pulling back his foot.

The youth stood over Nobby. 'Bet you can't go off the top board,' he growled.

Nobby could never refuse a challenge. 'Bet I could,' he said automatically, but when he looked up at the top board, he was visibly shaken. 'I . . . I bet you couldn't go off.'

The youth sneered. 'I could if you could,' he said.

'Go on then,' said Nobby eagerly.

'I asked you first.'

Nobby gulped with fear.

'I dare you,' repeated the urchin. 'You won't, 'cos you're scared.'

'No, I'm not,' said Nobby, hotly. He looked up at the board again and shivered. 'Besides, we aren't allowed to go off.'

The urchin sensed his fear and laughed.

'Chicken! Cubs are cissies.'

Snowy felt the hairs on the back of his neck bristle. His fists clenched up in indignation. It was with the greatest of difficulty that he restrained himself from starting an argument. Nobby, however, got up, walked around to the diving-tower, and began to climb the steps. Snowy was afraid for him. He knew Nobby could not swim. He also knew that Nobby had to sort out this problem himself. Nevertheless he went to the bottom of the tower to be ready to give any assistance should Nobby get into difficulties.

Nobby reached the top of the tower and walked along the board as gingerly as a man on a tight-rope. He hesitated at the end, half turned to come back, but dithered, utterly confused. This was not like spontaneous Nobby. He was scared stiff! He wrestled with the conflict in his mind.

He must have dithered on the edge of the board for fully five minutes. Suddenly Akela noticed him.

'Nobby!' he yelled up in anger. 'Come down from there at once.'

Nobby looked down. 'Come down?'

'Yes, come down, at once.'

Nobby closed his eyes, nipped his nose and stepped off the board. He came down like a bomb, and plunged into the water. Immediately Snowy was in the water beside him, to give him a hand to reach the side. No sooner had they reached the side, when Akela was on the scene. He grabbed Nobby by the arm and yanked him out of the water.

'Didn't I tell you to keep out of the deep end?'

Nobby stood on the side, dripping water. He looked up at Akela with innocent eyes. He pointed to the water, then up to the top diving-board'

'I wasn't in the deep end!' he said. 'I was up there. You told me to come down.'

But Akela was not going to twist words with him. He pointed to the dressing-room.

'Get dressed at once,' he said, firmly. 'Don't let me see you in this pool again today, or you'll be for it.'

Nobby turned meekly and went away. He seemed relieved to go. Akela stalked back to keep an eye on the Cubs splashing about in the shallow end.

Snowy climbed out of the pool, angry that his pal, Nobby, had had to make himself unpopular with Akela. He looked around for the urchin who had been the cause of all this trouble. The urchin caught his eye, and turned and walked away. Snowy went after him. The urchin walked around the back of the

kiddies' paddling-pool, and nipped through the arch
in a cypress hedge. Snowy slipped round the back of
the hedge to intercept him. He found the urchin
hiding behind a bush.

'Running away?' said Snowy, cutting off his retreat.

The urchin jumped. 'Mind your own business,' he
said, pushing his way past.

Snowy stood his ground.

'Now it's your turn to go off the top board.'

'No, no, no,' said the urchin, stricken with fear.

Snowy was so surprised that he let him pass. For a
moment he was tempted to shout 'Coward!' after
him, but he realized that was an idiotic thing to do.
To make anyone do something he was frightened to
do was just asking for trouble. Snowy shrugged his
shoulders and returned to the pool.

He was just in time. Nobby had dressed and had
joined the others on the lawn by the pool, and Akela
said they could all have a lemonade. The Cubs got
their drinks and gathered round Nobby to hear his
account of his death-defying leap.

'There I was,' said Nobby. 'Forty thousand feet,
coming down at Mach 2·5 . . .'

But Snowy was not listening. Beyond Nobby's
shoulder, he saw the urchin climb the diving-tower.
He watched, fascinated. The boy walked to the end
of the top board, hesitated, and Snowy could imagine

the torment in his mind, but the boy took a deep breath, closed his eyes and jumped. He came down like a shot pheasant, limbs outstretched for air which did not support him. He plunged beneath the water. Snowy watched, and it seemed an awful long time for the boy to surface, but when he did, he was floating face down.

Snowy jumped up in alarm, and saw the boy roll on to his back and let out what can only be described as an awful, desperate cry for help.

'Help! Hel-l-l-p!' he burbled, before rolling over and going under again.

'There's a boy in trouble,' shouted Snowy.

Akela pricked his ears. But the pool attendant, who

was walking past at the time, heard him too. He dropped his bucket and mop, and although fully clothed, dived in. Akela, Snowy and the other Cubs who realized what was up, rushed to the scene, where they helped the pool attendant and the boy out of the pool. The attendant sat the boy on the side of the pool. The boy was blue in the face. He coughed violently.

'What made you go off the top board, lad?' said the pool attendant.

'I . . . I just wanted to see if I could do it,' said the boy.

'But you can't swim.'

'I know,' said the boy, coughing violently, 'but I thought I could stretch out and reach the side.'

The pool attendant helped the boy to his feet.

'Well, you've got guts, that I can say for you, lad. That's probably the bravest thing I've ever seen since I left the army. Now come and get dressed.' The pool attendant turned to Akela. 'He's all right now, I'll look after him.'

With that, the pool attendant put his arm round the boy's shoulder and led him towards the changing rooms. Akela scratched his head, and looked at Nobby.

'It's all your fault,' he said.

'Mine?' said Nobby, innocently. 'I didn't touch him.'

'You're the very plague itself. Wherever you go, you spread infection. If you jumped in a river, there'd be a dozen fools like you who'd jump in with you. Oh, I give up. Back to the lawn to finish off your lemonade.'

The Cubs went back to their picnic spot to sunbathe. After about five minutes, the pool attendant, now in a dry tracksuit and plimsolls, came across to see Akela.

'The boy's all right now,' he said, 'but that's the bravest thing I've ever seen a boy of his age do. He has a hard life, that young 'un. His father is in prison, his mother doesn't want to know him, and nobody else wants to know him either. He's always getting himself in trouble, but he's got guts as you saw for yourself.'

Akela nodded. The pool attendant was excited.

'You've got to have guts to go off a high diving board, I know; I was a high diver myself once,' he continued. 'My championship days are over now, but he's just the lad I've been looking for to coach as a high diver. To go off that top board, not being able to swim, proves the lad has nerves of steel. I've seen many kids jump off the top board before, but none that could not swim. With my experience, and his youth and courage, I could make an Olympic champion of him. There'll be no one in the world to touch him when I've finished with him.'

Akela nodded. 'I hope you can,' he said. 'The boy needs a break like that, and as you say, he's got the guts to make a success of his life.'

'Aye, we'll see him a champion yet.'

The pool attendant picked up his bucket and mop and went back into the main building. Akela turned back to his Cubs. He noticed some of them were turning red in the sun.

'Right, Cubs, time to get dressed before you all turn into lobsters. In the showers first. Come on. Last one dressed is a cissy.'

Akela led the Cubs back to the changing-rooms. Snowy lingered, and looked up at the top board. It had an unusual fascination for him, it was so high.

He looked around. Neither Akela nor the pool attendant was in sight, and on a sudden impulse he walked towards the diving-tower. He climbed the first few steps. A sudden fear gripped him, but he forced himself to go on. His legs felt like lead, and he found he could not climb, but he used his arms to heave himself up the steps. After twenty vertical steps, he reached the top board, and with legs like jelly he walked along to the edge. He wanted to go back, and cursed himself for being so foolish as to come this far, but he knew the shame of going back would be worse than all the pain he would suffer going on. From the edge of the diving-board, he could see the pool, far, far below, like a tiny blue bath, and he was afraid he might miss it if he went off. But he also realized that even if he did drop in the water, he must plunge in cleanly, otherwise the impact with the water, hard as concrete, would rip him open. He wanted to go back, but he forced himself to go on. He leaned forward and felt he was about to fall. It was too late to go back now, impossible, but he did not know whether to leap or dive. He held his body straight, swung down and left the board.

Slowly he turned through the air until he was pointing straight down. He hurtled downwards with all the power of a railway express, and plunged into the water like a bullet. Still he continued to go down, down under the water. He twisted his body to surface, and after what seemed to be an age of coming up in a lift, in which he could not breathe, he broke the surface and gulped in a lungful of fresh air. It was a relief that it was all over. He swam to the side. When he climbed out, his legs were shaking, and it was with difficulty that he managed to walk back to the changing-rooms.

'Where have you been?' said Akela, sternly.

'Oh . . . oh, I've just had another quick dip.'

'Hurry up and get changed,' said Akela.

Snowy showered and dressed and realized that compared to himself, Nobby and the young urchin had indeed nerves of steel. They hadn't been able to swim. He knew from his own experience that the boy had the courage it takes to be an Olympic high diver.

After they had all dressed, they turned to leave. Snowy noticed the boy sitting with his new trainer in the entrance hall, looking at photographs of high divers. Snowy butted in.

'Best of luck with your diving training,' he said to the boy as he passed.

'Er, oh, thanks,' said the boy.

The pool attendant smiled. 'He'll be a champion yet, mark my words.'

'I hope so,' said Snowy. ''Bye!'

''Bye!' said the boy, surprised that someone had spoken kindly to him.

Snowy joined Nobby and the others in the Scout mini-bus.

'Hey, Nobby, how would you like to be a high-diving champion?' said Snowy.

'Not me,' said Nobby, modestly. 'Once is enough for me. I don't fancy being a human bomb again.'

Akela checked that all his Cubs were present and drove off for home. It had been an interesting day. Perhaps too, it was an important day, for they may have helped, in some small way, in the making of a champion.

3 · Snowy dials 999 . . .

THE mini-bus swerved in the gravel of The County Inn forecourt and skidded to a halt. The 2nd Billington Cubs looked out of their windows at the richly wooded countryside which surrounded the old inn.

'We're not going to camp here in a pub, are we?' asked Nobby.

'Not in the pub, Nobby,' said Akela, climbing out of his driving-seat and opening the door, 'but our camping site is not too far away, only two or three minutes' walk. My old Scoutmaster used to bring me here when I was a lad. We had some good times, I can tell you. Come on, get out, this is a camp outing, not a coach tour.'

The Cubs piled out into the bright sunshine which scorched the gravelled forecourt. Akela opened the boot of the mini-bus and handed out their camping gear.

'As you can see, we have brought along with us a fair amount of kit, too much really for a day's camping, but it will give you the opportunity to see how to set up a camp for a longer stay. Now, apart from the food, water and cooking utensils, you will also see that I've brought along the first aid kit. This is not because I expect any of you will have an accident – far from it – but I want to take this opportunity to show you what to do in a real emergency. After we have set up camp, we'll pretend one of you has a broken leg, and we will practise first aid, right? Give a hand to carry the kit.'

The Cubs picked up the equipment as Akela locked the boot. Nobby hitched a knapsack on his back. In it were the food rations for the party.

'Will the one who carries the sausages get an extra one for dinner?' he asked.

'No, he won't,' said Akela. 'All you think about is feeding your face. Everyone gets the same on an outing when I'm in charge. Right, Pack, off we go.'

Akela led his Cubs along a narrow footpath which disappeared into the woods behind the old inn.

'Is it . . . is it all right to leave the mini-bus?' asked Snowy, steadying a side-pack on his hip.

'Yes, I have permission,' said Akela. 'Until seven o'clock, that is. The camp is only a hundred metres down this path, beside a little gully.'

The path turned off into a grassy clearing which was to be their camp. The Cubs dropped their kit and Akela showed them how to set up their tent. He also showed them how to make a camp fire, by lighting, with a match, a pile of the smallest twigs his Cubs could find, and using that to light increasingly bigger twigs which he carefully piled on top. Within minutes, he had a sizeable wood fire going.

The Cubs, although each had helped in some way to set up the camp, still had plenty of energy. Akela had forbidden them to bring a ball with them, but there were many other games they could play. They played 'touch-and-go' which they called 'tiggy'. In this game, one Cub had to touch or tigg any Cub he could, and once 'tigged', that Cub had to catch and tigg another Cub, et cetera.

Nobby was tigged by Louie, and in an attempt to chase Whippet he tripped over a rock and fell flat on his face. He wasn't seriously hurt, but he had a cut on his knee and the blood flowed quite freely. Akela then thought it was time to call a halt to the boisterous game, and took the opportunity to use Nobby's grazed knee as an excuse to demonstrate the art of first aid. He showed them how to clean and dress the wound, with Nobby sitting on the rock, an innocent spectator. Soon Nobby had his knee neatly bandaged up.

All the Cubs were grateful to Nobby for grazing his knee, in fact Spotty suggested that it would have been even better had Nobby broken his arm, smashed

open his head and burnt his hands, then they could
have a much better demonstration of first aid. Nobby
was reluctant to oblige them, but Akela said it didn't
matter, for they could pretend Nobby had broken his
arm, smashed open his head and burnt his hands, and
then gave a demonstration of what he would do in the
circumstances. First he bandaged up Nobby's head,
then he bandaged up Nobby's hands, then he applied
splints to Nobby's arm, and put the arm in a sling.
Akela even showed his Cubs what to do with a
broken leg, if they found themselves without splints,
by strapping the supposedly broken leg firmly to the
good leg.

'That's a demonstration of first aid,' summarized Akela. 'Are you comfortable, Nobby?'

Nobby nodded, but he could not reply because the bandages round his chin restricted his jaw movements.

'If Nobby was so badly injured, our next job would be to get him to a hospital, where he could have more elaborate treatment. Let me show you how to make a rough stretcher from a blanket and –'

But Akela was not to finish his demonstration. Snowy heard a shout and turned to see a youth stumbling along the gully.

'Can you come and help my brother,' he gasped at Akela. He pointed back up the gully. 'A machine's fallen on him in the woodyard. Come quickly, he's badly hurt.'

Akela jumped up. 'Snowy, Bobbie, come with me. The rest of you stay here. Don't lark about or else I'll be very angry when I get back.'

Akela scooped up the first aid side-pack.

'He's along here,' said the youth, turning to go back along the gully.

'Lead the way,' said Akela.

The rescue party ran as fast as they could. After about a minute of slithering and stumbling along the rocky gully, they came to the back of a woodyard. There Snowy saw a conveying-machine which had collapsed on top of a boy of about ten, just a couple of years younger than his brother. The ten-year-old was crying with pain. Akela knelt beside him, gripped the metal sides of the conveying-machine and strained to lift it.

'We . . . were only trying to get it started so we could have a ride,' said the older boy.

Akela ignored him. 'Snowy, go back to the camp and tell all the Cubs to come here and help me lift this conveyor, then go on to the inn and telephone an ambulance. Bobbie, go with him and lead the Cubs back here.'

The two Sixers dashed away to do what they were told. Snowy left Bobbie to cope with the rest of the Cubs, and ran on as fast as he could to The County Inn. He barged through the swing doors and, to his utmost relief, saw a telephone in the hall.

'You can't come in here,' said a barman in the hall.

Snowy grabbed the telephone from its cradle. 'It's an emergency,' he said. 'Two boys playing on a machine in the woodyard – one of them is injured.'

'Not the Kelly scallywags!' said the barman. 'They are always in trouble.'

Snowy dialled 999.

'Can you use the telephone?' asked the barman.

Snowy nodded. The barman dropped his cloth and dashed out through the swing doors.

'Emergency; which service do you require?' said the calm voice of the telephone operator. 'Ambulance, police or fire-brigade?'

'Ambulance!' said Snowy.

'Putting you through.'

'Ambulance service,' said a man's voice.

'There's been an accident,' said Snowy. 'I want an ambulance.'

'Where are you?' asked the voice.

'I'm speaking from The County Inn. It's on the Runcorn–Northwich road, A533 I think it's called.'

'I know it,' said the voice. 'Go on, sonny.'

'There has been an accident in the woodyard not

far from this old inn. I don't think you can drive there, I mean I don't know if you can, but if you park at The County Inn, I can show you a short cut through the woods.'

'There's an ambulance on its way now. Meet it at the inn, and show the ambulance men the way. Can you do that?'

'Yes, I'll meet them in the forecourt.'

'Good boy, now before you go, tell me about the accident.'

'A boy, about ten years old, was hurt when a conveying-machine fell on him. Akela, my Cub Scout Leader is with him now, giving him first aid. Akela knows all about first aid. He won't let the boy die . . . but hurry, please hurry.'

'Don't worry about that, sonny. My men will be there within a few minutes . . .'

'I'll . . . I'll wait outside for them.'

Snowy put down the receiver, straightened his scarf and cap and went outside into the bright sunshine. There was no traffic on the road. It was a quiet day, calm and still. It was very difficult to imagine that a boy, not far away, desperately needed help. Snowy positioned himself near the entrance to the forecourt, so he could see both ways along the road.

A sportscar raced by, then a tractor, then Snowy

heard the wailing klaxon of the ambulance. The white vehicle, lights flashing, swung into the forecourt as Snowy waved it down.

'Where's the accident?' called the driver, leaning from his window, as two of his companions leapt out of the back of the vehicle with a stretcher.

'In the woodyard,' said Snowy, pointing along the track. 'A hundred metres down this path and a little way up the gully. My Cub Scout Leader is giving him first aid now.'

The stretcher-bearers dashed off down the track. They shot away so fast that they practically disappeared in front of his eyes.

'How did it happen?' said the ambulance driver, jumping out of his vehicle.

'I don't know, really. All I saw was this long conveying-machine lying across the boy's back. Akela got the Cubs to give him a hand to lift the machine. He's there with our first aid kit.'

'Show me!' said the ambulance driver.

'It's along here.'

Snowy led the way down the path. All the way the ambulance driver kept him talking so he could find out as much as possible about the accident. They had almost reached the gully when they saw the stretcher-bearers hurrying back.

'Multiple injuries!' shouted the leading stretcher-bearer. 'Back to hospital at the double, or we'll lose him.'

The ambulance driver turned and ran back to his vehicle, followed by the stretcher-bearers who raced past Snowy like an express train. Snowy glimpsed the still body beneath the grey-brown hospital blanket, and for a moment was uncertain whether to follow or go back to Akela. But his mind was soon made up for him. The ambulance men slid their patient into the back of the vehicle, slammed the doors and raced off with klaxon blaring and lights flashing. Snowy shrugged his shoulders and went back to find the others. The 2nd Billingtons had done what they could in the emergency. It was up to the hospital staff to save the boy now.

Snowy was a little surprised not to find his pal Nobby still in the camp, but he guessed he must have torn off his bandages and gone off to the woodyard with the others to help Akela. So Snowy made his own way back up the gully. In the woodyard he saw his fellow Cubs, Akela, the County Inn barman and two other boys. Two other boys! One was the youth who had called for assistance, the other was the boy he had seen under the conveying-machine. Snowy blinked and came into the woodyard to get a better look. The conveying-machine was now upright, and beside it was Akela talking to the ten-year-old boy.

'Silly thing to do,' said Akela casually. 'You might have been seriously injured. Not many people would have been as lucky as you to get away without a mark on your body.'

'We were only playing,' said his elder brother.

'If I was your father, I'd give both of you such a good hiding that you'd never want to touch another thing which wasn't yours,' said the barman. 'What's the matter with you? Haven't you got anything better to do? I thought you got a guitar last Christmas. What's the matter with that? Have you got fed up with it?'

'Ah, a string broke,' grunted the older boy.

'String broke?' scoffed the barman. 'I really don't know . . .'

Akela turned as Snowy approached.

'We won't be needing an ambulance after all, Snowy,' he said. 'Did you have any trouble getting through?'

Snowy gulped. 'They've been. They've gone. They took away somebody on a stretcher. I think it was Nobby.'

'Nobby!' shrieked Akela. 'He hasn't been in an accident, has he?'

'No, but we left him all bandaged up. I think they've taken him away to hospital.'

'Nobby didn't ask to be taken to hospital, did he?' asked Akela, utterly confused by the turn of events.

'N– no,' said Snowy. 'He couldn't speak, with all those bandages around his head.'

'Oooooh!' gasped Akela. 'Wait until I get my hands on that little wretch. I'll . . . I'll skin him alive.'

'I don't think Nobby wanted to be taken to hospital at all,' said Snowy in his pal's defence. 'I don't think Nobby could say anything.'

Akela stormed off to the telephone to tell the

ambulance service they had made a terrible mistake in taking away Nobby. However, no harm was done. When the hospital doctor undressed Nobby's slings, splints and bandages, he was surprised to see the little boy was all in one piece. The hospital promised to deliver Nobby to Cub headquarters by staff car as soon as it could be arranged.

So Akela had to return without Nobby, but he was, as much as anyone, relieved when Nobby was safely delivered to Cub headquarters by a doctor who had just come off duty. Nobby seemed none the worse for his experience.

'He nearly caused a riot in the hospital,' said the doctor.

'I'm not surprised,' said Akela. 'He causes riots everywhere.'

'As soon as we took off his dressings,' went on the doctor, 'he leapt off the table and scampered out of the casualty ward before we could stop him. We chased him all round the isolation ward and caught him hiding in the linen cupboard.'

'Nobby!' said Akela, sternly.

'Well, I thought they were going to give me a heart transplant,' said Nobby, not at all amused.

Akela glowered at him. 'Pity they didn't give you a head transplant,' he said.

4 · The old mill story

AKELA led the 2nd Billington Cub Scout Pack over the wooden footbridge which crossed the gushing little stream to a neat green lawn before the old mill. Some of the Cubs stopped on the footbridge to watch the water driving the mill-wheel. Snowy found moving water fascinating to watch. The stream danced with carefree life.

'No larking about,' growled Akela, cautiously. 'If any of you should fall in, you'd be mashed up by the mill-wheel before you'd have time to say "corned beef". In fact you would be corned beef before you'd have time to say "corned beef".'

But Akela let his Cubs take their time to watch the bubbling stream, for they were in no real danger. The footbridge itself was in good repair, with stout rails on either side, so that no one who did not deliberately wish to commit suicide would be in any danger of falling in. When the Cubs had satisfied their immediate curiosity, they came on to the lawn to look at the old mill itself, which was now converted into a neat little café.

'Did you know this place sells lemonade?' Nobby hinted, wiping his hot face down with the ends of his scarf. 'I'm . . . I'm on the point of dying with thirst.'

'Wait a minute, wait a minute, wait a minute, guzzleguts!' said Akela. 'All in good time. If you really are so thirsty, you can have a capful of cool, clear water from the stream.'

'Capful?' said Nobby. 'You mean cupful, don't you? I'm . . . I'm not wearing a cup on my head.'

'If that's all you can say, you are obviously not dying of thirst, so shut up and listen to what I have to say.'

The Cubs gathered round their Cub Scout Leader to hear what he had to say. They sensed he was about to tell them another of his fascinating stories.

'Local history,' said Akela. 'Now what's the use of local history? you may ask. Well, I'll tell you. There are many interesting places within a short distance of where you live, and associated with these places are stories, true stories, of what happened to people who were here years, even centuries ago. If you know these stories, and know the places where these stories happened, you can have a very vivid idea of what people were like in times gone by. If you can understand what life used to be like, you will find your local area so much more interesting that you will want to improve the area whenever you can, and help the people who still live here. It makes life so much more real. That's why I've brought you here today.'

Nobby looked behind him at the neat little white café.

'What's a pop-shop got to do with local history?' he asked.

'That pop-shop, as you call it, was originally built as a mill, before they had all these new-fangled automatic plants which turn grain into flour,' said Akela. 'In the old days, the water in this stream used to turn the mill-wheel, which used to turn a mill-stone inside the building, which used to rub against a stationary stone to grind the grains of wheat sprinkled between the stones into flour, so the people could make bread.'

Nobby looked again at the neat little white café. 'I didn't know they made their own flour in there.'

'They don't now,' said Akela. 'When they stopped making flour, the building was converted into this modern café.'

'Oh!'

'If you file into the shop in a civilized manner,' went on Akela, 'you can each have a lemonade.'

The Cubs filed into the café, and were at once fascinated by the place. The café itself was furnished

in a style which was as up-to-date as anything they
had seen anywhere in the county. But what was
much more interesting was the original milling
machinery, which had been overhauled, and was
complete apart from the pair of mill-stones. The
machinery was visible through an open doorway at
the side of the serving-bar. The open doorway was

partially screened by a metre-high wire-mesh safety fence. It was a necessary safeguard, for the giant cogs and gear wheels, which were still turning majestically under the power of the mill stream, could easily catch and crush anything which came between them. For one awful moment, Snowy imagined a body caught between the revolving gears. The gears would probably jam, but without doubt the unfortunate body would be crushed to death.

'Just the thing for cracking nuts,' said Nobby. 'Coconuts.'

'Are you thinking of putting your head between the gears?' said Akela.

'I'd rather keep my head between my ears,' said Nobby.

'Move on and let someone else see.'

The Cubs moved along to the bar where they bought their lemonades. Apart from the high stools at the bar, tables and chairs were set out, but as the weather was so fine the Cubs decided to drink their lemonade outside, on the lawn. There were other people there too, enjoying the sunshine.

Akela gathered his Cubs around. 'There is another story to this mill,' he said. 'Before the Napoleonic war, when this old mill was still grinding out its flour, a boy called Jack Palmer lived here.'

Immediately in Snowy's mind the name rang a bell.

'Palmer of the Nile,' he said.

'Who?' said Nobby.

'Jack Palmer,' said Snowy. 'You know. There's a statue of him in the park, nailing a flag on to a broken mast. He was a cabin-boy in Nelson's day, and there's a picture of him and his gold medal in the museum.'

'Ah!' said Nobby.

'The same,' said Akela. 'The boy joined the navy when he was fourteen, as a cabin-boy. In 1798, whilst on duty in the frigate HMS *Fleetwing*, he was in action against the French at the Battle of the Nile. The French flagship, *Triomphe* shot away the British frigate's ensign in the battle. Young Jack Palmer immediately took up the flag, and with a marlin spike, that is a piece of iron used for splicing ropes, he nailed the flag on the mizzen mast although the shot was flying round him all the time. *Fleetwing* had been badly knocked about, but the courageous action of the boy inspired his shipmates to fight on, so much so that they later boarded the Frenchman and captured her. The action of young Jack, on his first trip to sea, had literally turned defeat into victory.'

'And he actually lived here?' asked Snowy.

'Yes, nearly two hundred years ago. And it isn't very difficult, if you try, to imagine that young boy sailing a little model boat in this stream, as he must have done at one time or other.'

Snowy liked that story. Of course England and France would never have another war, yet the actions of the men and boys who sailed in the old fighting-ships, still stirred him. The story had, as Akela had forecast, made him feel closer to his home and the people who lived in the area.

'The café's still called Palmer's,' said Snowy.

'The same family,' said Akela.

By some strange chance, a six- or seven-year-old youngster was sailing a model boat in the waters of the dammed-up stream. Perhaps he was standing in the very same footprints of the young naval hero of long ago.

When the Cubs had finished their lemonade, Snowy and Nobby helped collect the empty bottles to return them to the café. They were just about to go through the door of the café when Snowy heard a shout. He turned and realized that the young boy had fallen into the stream, and because of the steep banks no one was in a position to reach him, and he was being swept to the dam. In a few seconds, Snowy saw he would be swept over the dam into the mill-wheel. He would be crunched to death!

Immediately Snowy dropped the lemonade bottles and barged into the café, hoping to find a way to stop the wheel before an awful tragedy occurred. He saw the huge gears grinding away behind the counter.

Snowy yelled a warning, but nobody paid any attention to him.

Sitting on the stool by the bar counter, with her back to him, was a large, stout woman, sipping a strawberry soda. Snowy charged at her, having no time for civilized courtesies. He butted her in the small of the back, and knocked her clean off the stool so she spilt her strawberry soda down her dress. Then completely ignoring her screams of abuse, he picked up her stool, ran to the entrance of the grinding-room, and hurled the stool between the gears of the mighty wheels. The gears smashed up the stool like matchwood, but were jammed in the process. The mill-wheel had stopped.

Snowy turned to see the fat lady beating Nobby over the head with her umbrella.

'Take that, you horrible young hooligan,' said the fat lady. 'How dare you knock me off that stool? You spilt my strawberry soda down my new yellow dress.'

'It wasn't me, it wasn't me,' yelled Nobby, trying to fight her off with his cap.

The fat lady gave Nobby another painful whack, then she advanced on Snowy.

'There's a child in the stream under the mill-wheel,' shouted Snowy, putting up an arm to protect himself from the raised umbrella.

The umbrella stopped in mid-air. The lady listened

to the noise and shouts outside and dashed out to find
out what the commotion was all about. Snowy and
Nobby followed, in time to see the boy being lifted
out from beneath the stationary mill-wheel by Akela.

The boy had had a lucky escape. The wheel had
stopped only just in time, but he recovered quickly

enough when he was back with his parents. His parents took him to their car to dry him, and no doubt to make sure he didn't get out of their sight again in a hurry.

Snowy's legs still felt like jelly, for he could not get out of his imagination the terrible tragedy which had just been averted. But all was well, and Akela was the first to pull himself together. He even laughed with relief.

'Well, Cubs,' said Akela, 'we are fortunate today in seeing a bit of local history made. The story of Snowy's quick action will last a hundred years, longer. As long as this old mill stands, this story will live. We are part of a legend which may live for a thousand years.'

'A thousand years?' said Nobby, glumly.

'Wouldn't you like to be remembered for a thousand years?' asked Akela. 'Don't you want to be part of history?'

'I don't mind being part of history,' said Nobby, 'but how will I be remembered in a thousand years, eh? I'll tell you. In a thousand years' time, I'll be remembered as the boy who was whacked with an umbrella by a fat lady!'

5 · Test match

PACK outings were always great fun, and when for their next Pack outing the Cubs of the 2nd Billington Cub Scout Pack learnt that Akela was taking them to Old Trafford to see the test match between England and Australia, their joy knew no bounds.

The match itself was adequately covered in the newspapers at the time, and is, of course, permanently recorded in cricket histories, along with other matches. Since it is impossible to compete with the sports writers, who have done their jobs so well, it is unwise to go into the statistics of the game in this book, which after all, is merely the story of the experiences of two Cubs in the 2nd Billington Cub Scout Pack. But, of the match, one fact was outstanding. Roy Hudson played a superb innings.

Roy Hudson was an eighteen-year-old Somerset man, playing his first test innings. He opened for England. Going out to bat against the Australians, though thrilling, must be one of the most terrifying of all human experiences. It was not a batsman's wicket. It was a fast wicket, and the Australians knew it. They brought what newspapers described as 'the two fastest bowlers in the world' into action against the new man. The crowd expected to see the stumps flying.

But Roy Hudson stood his ground for the first few overs to judge the opposition, then he made the crowd gasp by actually going out from the wicket to meet the fast bowling. He played a variety of strokes, every stroke in the book, and more besides. He cut, drove, turned and glanced the ball all around the clock. He immediately became Snowy's hero, and of all Hudson's strokes, the one Snowy liked best was where the batsman went down the pitch with his bat over his head like a golf club, to half-volley the ball over the sightscreen.

Snowy memorized the whole graceful movement of the stroke, until he moved in his imagination with the batsman. By lunchtime, Hudson had got his fifty. In an hour, this unknown young man had become a cricketing legend.

The crowd flocked to the pavilion to give the young player a standing ovation as he came in. Much as he wanted to rush forward, Snowy stood well back, knowing he would have no chance of seeing his hero in that crowd. Then something quite different caught his eye.

As the hero-worshipping crowd surged forward to see the incoming players, they squeezed up together. At the back of the crowd was a slim, hungry-looking man, who took no interest at all in the spectacle which held the rest of the crowd spellbound. The slim man deliberately lifted up the back hem of the blazer of the man in front, and slipped his wallet from his hip pocket.

The man was a pickpocket! Snowy could hardly believe his eyes. The pickpocket turned and walked quickly away, with his head down and his coat collar up, as if he didn't want to be recognized.

Snowy looked around for Akela or for an official to warn. Akela was at the front of the pavilion, pulling back a couple of his Cubs, Whippet and Louie, who were trying to climb through the pavilion railings. Snowy had no time to reach him and point out the pickpocket.

'Come with me, Nobby,' said Snowy quickly. 'That man's a pickpocket. We've got to keep an eye on him.'

'Pickpocket? Where?' said Nobby, looking round. 'I can't see any pickpockets.'

'Don't argue. Come with me.'

Snowy had to run after the pickpocket to keep him in sight. The man slipped and weaved through the crowd like a snake. On one occasion, Snowy lost sight

of him completely, but he reappeared again. This time he had turned down his coat collar and had taken off his cap, but Snowy immediately recognized his characteristic walk, head down, body forward, hands in pockets, and went after him. The pickpocket was heading for the main gates.

'Wait a minute, wait a minute,' said Nobby, running hard to keep up with Snowy. 'Where are we going? You know Akela said we weren't to go off without his permission.'

'Keep going, Nobby. I'll . . . I'll explain later.'

As Snowy had expected, the pickpocket slipped

through the main gate. The Cubs went through after him. The pickpocket half turned and saw a double-decker bus pull in to a bus stop. He jumped on board and slipped upstairs. The Cubs jumped on board just as the bus moved off, went upstairs and got a seat behind the pickpocket.

Snowy hadn't the faintest idea where he was going. This was the first time he had ever been to Manchester, and Manchester was a very large, bustling city. Snowy was completely lost.

'Piccadilly,' said the pickpocket to the conductor, when he came to collect the fares.

'Two halves to Piccadilly,' said Snowy, not knowing where or what Piccadilly was.

The pickpocket took a wallet, the stolen wallet, from his pocket, and extracted a wad of pound notes. He put the wallet and notes in separate pockets. When the bus reached the city centre, he slipped the wallet out of his pocket and dropped it down the side of his seat, then he stood up and went downstairs to get off the bus.

Snowy whipped out his handkerchief and used it to pick up the wallet without leaving his finger-prints on it. Then he and Nobby went down after the pickpocket. The pickpocket jumped off the bus and slipped into the saloon bar of a corner public house. Being under age, the Cubs could not follow him.

They were stranded in the centre of Manchester, feeling they had not a friend in the world.

Snowy looked around for a policeman, but the only one he could see was one on traffic duty on an island in the middle of the road. The policeman put up his hands to stop the traffic. When the traffic had stopped, he turned and beckoned the crowd of city shoppers to cross the road. Snowy pulled Nobby across with the crowd.

'There's a pickpocket in that public house,' said Snowy to the traffic policeman on the island.

'Stand there and don't move,' said the traffic policeman, making room for them on the island.

When the crowd had crossed over, the policeman put up his hand to stop any late-comers trying to cross over, then he waved on the traffic on both sides of the island.

'I . . . I didn't want to interfere with your traffic duties, but you were the only policeman in sight, and . . . and I had to tell someone before the pickpocket got away.'

'How do you know he's a pickpocket?' said the policeman casually, paying more attention to the traffic than to the boys.

'I . . . I saw him pick a man's pocket at Old Trafford cricket ground. We followed him here. He went into that public bar.'

'Oh?' said the policeman. 'Well, we must do something about that, mustn't we?'

The policeman continued to wave on the traffic with one hand, then with the other hand, he took a radio unit from the inside of his tunic.

'47 to Control,' he said.

'Go ahead, 47,' came a voice.

'47. I've a couple of Cub Scouts with me, who think they saw a pickpocket enter the "Rose and Crown" I'm on traffic duty in Piccadilly, so I'm unable to investigate this matter. Send a car, will you?'

'Will do,' said the controller.

The policeman switched off his radio and slipped it back into his tunic, then he put up his hand to stop the traffic.

'Now you two, I want you to go and stand in that shop doorway until we get a police officer to attend to you, right?'

Snowy nodded. The policeman then waved the pedestrians across the street, and Snowy and Nobby went across to the shop to wait for the police reinforcements. They gazed in the shop window.

'Whee! Look at all those model aircraft,' said Nobby. 'There's a radio-controlled triplane. And there's a model of the Royal Flying Doctor's aircraft. Wow, if I had that, I'd send it up, zoom it over the scene of some accident and drop bandages on little parachutes to the casualties. Hey, that's a good idea, we could get a squadron of those aircraft, ready to fly off at a moment's notice to any emergency to drop supplies. And when they were not on duty, they could keep in practice by flying over Cub headquarters and dropping sweets and chocolate on us to keep us from starving. If we made Akela the Squadron Leader, he could supply the sweets and chocolates . . .'

Snowy gazed at the model aircraft, but he found he could not concentrate on them. His mind kept turning to the pickpocket, and he knew that as time went by it would be more difficult to catch the offender. But the quick arrival of the police surprised him. He sensed someone was behind him, and when he turned he saw three policemen towering over him.

'Now what's all this about a pickpocket?' said a policeman.

'I saw him take a wallet from a spectator in Old Trafford cricket ground,' said Snowy. 'We followed him here in the bus, and he took the money out of the wallet and dropped the wallet down the side of the bus seat.' Snowy showed the policeman the wallet. 'This is the wallet. I . . . I picked it up with my handkerchief so as not to leave my finger-prints.'

The policeman took the wallet. 'And where is this . . . pickpocket now?'

'In that public house,' said Snowy, pointing to the saloon bar entrance.

'Come and show us the man.'

'But . . . but . . . but we aren't allowed to go in public houses,' said Snowy, hesitating.

'We'll make a special allowance this time,' said the policeman, taking Snowy by the hand. 'Come along now.'

They went into the saloon bar, with Snowy's heart beating wildly. He hoped he was still in time to catch the pickpocket. But he need not have worried, for there sitting at a corner table, reading a sporting paper, was the man he had followed from the cricket ground.

There was no need for Snowy to point him out, for the policeman recognized him immediately. He walked across to the corner table.

'Up to your old tricks again, Fingers?' said the policeman.

'What do you mean?' said Fingers in surprise. 'I've not done nothing. Can't a fellow have a quiet drink without being bothered by the law?'

The policeman dropped the wallet on the table. 'You never learn, do you? You've only been out of prison a week . . .'

Fingers glanced at the wallet then, in an uncontrollable rage, he clenched his first and lashed out at Nobby who was standing near him, knocking the

little boy half-way across the room. Immediately two policeman fell on the attacker, twisted his arms behind his back, and dragged him screaming and kicking out of the bar. The third policeman and Snowy went to Nobby's aid.

'How are you, young 'un?' asked the policeman.

Nobby shook his head. 'I feel as if I've been kicked by a horse.'

'You're a brave little 'un, aren't you? We won't let Fingers get away with this, you can be sure of that. Can you come down to the police station to make a statement?'

Nobby rubbed his sore jaw and nodded. 'I don't know where the police station is, but I'll come.'

'Good lad!'

So the Cubs were taken to the police station, where they gave and signed their statements. Then they were driven back to Old Trafford cricket ground, and so they wouldn't have to pay again to get in, the policeman took them through the players' entrance, and explained to the club secretary what had happened.

'I'm very pleased and relieved to hear you've caught the pickpocket,' said the club secretary. 'We've had a dozen complaints this last week. Anyone who helps catch a pickpocket deserves a free ticket. Come on through, boys.'

So the Cubs were allowed to go through the

pavilion to rejoin Akela and the other Cubs. Akela
had been forewarned that his two missing Cubs were
in safe hands, but he was waiting to give them a piece
of his mind.

'This is the end!' he said, angrily. 'There will be no
more Pack outings. How many times have I told you,
you must learn to stay with the Pack, and not go off
on your own without telling me . . .?'

'Their quick action did help catch the pickpocket,'
said the club secretary, trying to keep the peace. He
put his arm round Nobby's shoulder. 'I'd like you to
accept this old cricket ball in appreciation of what
you've done today.' He gave the ball to Nobby. 'It's a
bit knocked about, as Roy Hudson scored his century
from it, but it will be a priceless souvenir for anyone
interested in cricket. Roy Hudson has a promising
cricket career ahead of him, and it wouldn't surprise
me if he makes a real name for himself and for
English cricket.'

Nobby handed the ball to Akela.

'What do you expect me to do with this?' said
Akela. 'Bowl you a googly?'

'You can take it with us on the next Pack outing,'
said Nobby.

'I told you there'll be no more Pack outings. No
more, and that's definite!' Akela fingered the seam of
the cricket ball. 'Well – not this week, anyway!'

6 · Play the game

IT is becoming increasingly difficult to find a playing field for the odd game, but Akela, who knew the local area like the back of his hand, remembered a quiet little glade in the woods beyond the railway track. He hadn't been there for years, but he thought his Cubs would like to see it, and of course there he could teach them something of the noble art of cricket, in preparation for their Sportsman Badge.

'I like cricket,' said Akela, as he loaded the cricket gear into the boot of the Scout mini-bus. 'Cricket, like most other sports, is a healthy exercise. It gets you out in the fresh air, and gives you the opportunity to shake the stiffness out of your limbs, and builds up your bodies. The fast-moving ball develops your reactions and the quickness of your eye. And, being a team game, it helps to develop loyalty, friendship and sportsmanship. In cricket, you learn to take defeat like a man and victory like a gentleman. Besides, it's good fun, and I 'can't think of a better reason than that for wanting to play it.'

Akela loaded a rotary lawnmower in the boot, and a roll of coconut-matting. The Cubs then piled into the mini-bus, Akela checked that they were all present, closed the door, and drove off to his little glade.

The glade turned out to be a spot of calm beauty. The grassy clearing itself had a diameter of about fifty metres, and it was surrounded by tall beech and elm trees. Although the disused railway track was within range of a well-thrown cricket ball, it was so well screened that it might not have existed at all. The glade was spacious enough not be overpowering, but was so sheltered that there was no sign of man's concrete jungle. It was a little bit of unspoilt England.

'Nice spot, isn't it?' said Akela, as he let the Cubs out of the mini-bus. 'I was chased by a bull here when I was your age. I can't see it around today, so we can have our game of cricket without fear.'

'The grass is too long,' said Nobby.

'Little Nobby Give-Up-Quick!' said Akela. 'Why do you think I brought the lawnmower? Don't you know the Cub Scout motto is "Be Prepared"? If you waited around for someone to cut the grass for you, you could ask them to trim your beard at the same time. Give a hand to unload the gear.'

The Cubs unloaded the cricket gear with the speed of a National Life Boat crew. Akela, with his rotary lawnmower, cleared a three-metre-wide strip in the

centre of the clearing. Four stumps were knocked in the ground, three to make a wicket, and the other to mark the bowling end. In front of the wicket, Akela instructed the Cubs to lay down the strip of coconut-matting, to provide a bump free surface. Within minutes, the cricket ground was prepared. It was neither large nor elaborate enough for a serious game of cricket, but it was ideal for their purpose.

'Snowy and Bobbie, toss for sides and who bats first.'

The two Sixers picked their teams. They called themselves 'M.C.C.' and 'Australia'. Snowy, the 'M.C.C.' captain, put in 'Australia' to bat first. So the game proceeded, each side trying to win, with the determination of the test players they imagined themselves to be.

Snowy himself believed that concentration could make all the difference between winning and losing, and by keeping alert, and going after the slightest chance of making a catch, took three catches in the slips. This helped to put out the opposing side for 38. It was a low score by professional standards, but it would be difficult for another side of young Cubs to beat.

Snowy, opening for his side, immediately got off the mark with two quick singles. Then tragedy fell. Snowy knocked the next ball towards the boundary, and tried to score two runs. But the fielder was quick on the ball and sent back a fast return, just as Snowy was approaching his crease. The hard ball caught Snowy on his bare elbow. Snowy dropped his bat inside his mark and let out a yell of pain before he could control himself. Akela then immediately examined the injury and declared that there were no broken bones. However, the elbow was extremely painful, and much as he disliked the idea, Snowy was forced to retire. He joined the others of his side sitting beside the Scout mini-bus, to keep score.

It was then that Snowy noticed another spectator within a few paces of the Scout mini-bus. He was a heavily built, oldish man; he wore wellington boots in spite of the hot, sunny weather, and an old sports jacket. But he paid no attention to Snowy, or to the Cubs awaiting their turn to bat. He watched the game, leaning on his walking stick.

Snowy turned his attention to the score book. 'Australia' . . . 38 all out. 'M.C.C.' . . . 4 for 0. The game was wide open.

Then the 'M.C.C.' wickets began to go down: 4 for 1, 5 for 2, 10 for 3, 14 for 4, 18 for 5, 18 for 6, 19 for 7, 20 for 8, and a fine innings by Podge, the tail-ender, brought the score to 33 for 9.

'Are you fit enough to come back, Snowy?' asked Akela.

Snowy's elbow was still painful when he moved it, but he felt he could not let down his side by refusing to bat.

'I . . . I think so,' said Snowy.

'I'll run for you,' said Nobby, who had been put out for a duck. The little fool had caught himself out! He had nicked the ball straight up, caught it expertly with one hand and had thrown it back to the bowler. 'Bowl me a lower one next time,' he had said, 'and I'll knock it for six.'

'Howzat?. said the bowler.

'Out!' said Akela.

So Nobby was out for the grand total of nothing. Only Snowy could save his side now.

'My legs are all right,' said Snowy, 'but I'd appreciate your help, Nobby. I don't think I could carry a bat with my left hand and run as quickly as otherwise.'

So Snowy again faced the bowling with Nobby as his runner, about ten metres away on the off side. Snowy took up his stance.

The ball came down fast and straight for his wicket. Snowy stopped it, but so painful was his elbow that the bat was nearly knocked clean out of his hand. The same happened with the next ball. Snowy could play it no more than a couple of metres from his bat.

The 'Australian' fielders recognized his weakness and closed in. The next ball came down, fast, low and short, the sort of ball Snowy, in normal circumstances, could best play. Snowy gritted his teeth and, in spite of the pain, gripped his bat as firmly as he could, and lashed out – like Roy Hudson. He connected with the ball and sent it over the players' heads towards the boundary. The fielders turned and ran, not quite sure where the ball lay in the long grass.

'Run, Nobby,' shouted Snowy, trying to hold his painful elbow.

But Nobby was half-way down the pitch like a young hare.

'Don't call for a lost ball,' shouted Bobbie, the opposing captain, knowing that the resulting five runs would give Snowy's side the game.

All the fielders except the wicket-keeper searched the long grass for the ball while Nobby darted up and down the pitch. Nobby was going so fast that the scorer lost count of the runs. At one time, Nobby and Snowy's batting partner, little Whippet, were racing each other for the same crease.

'How many runs have you got?' asked Snowy, as Whippet came down the pitch for the third time.

'Five,' said Whippet.

'And I've run seven, which makes twelve,' said Nobby, 'so we've won.'

'Run another one,' said Snowy to Whippet.

'Are you trying to score a century?' said Nobby, sitting on his bat. 'I'm puffed. If you want another run, you can run it yourself.'

The fielders found the ball, but they were unable to prevent Whippet from running back to his crease, so officially Snowy's side won the game. They returned to the Scout mini-bus.

'I'm out of puff,' gasped Nobby, collapsing on the grass.

'Thanks, Nobby,' said Snowy. 'You saved the side.'

The Cubs had brought with them their camping gear so they set up a fire to brew a can of tea. Snowy got out the jam sandwiches, and as he handed them round, he noticed the stranger was watching him.

'Would you like a sandwich, mister?' he said, more out of politeness than a wish to befriend the intruder.

'Do you know this is my land?' said the stranger, abruptly.

Snowy shrugged his shoulders. 'I didn't know,' he said, 'but we'll be going in a few minutes. Would you like a sandwich?'

The stranger grunted and took a sandwich. Snowy returned to his group to collect a mug of tea. He quickly put the stranger out of his mind, until a big shadow fell across him. The stranger addressed himself to Akela.

'Do you know this is my land?' repeated the stranger. 'Did you see the "No Trespassing" sign?'

'I knew it must belong to someone, but I didn't know who,' said Akela, looking around. 'Do you want us to go?'

'No, no, no,' said the stranger. 'I didn't mean that. As a matter of fact, I just came to measure up the ground,' he said, half pulling a steel tape-measure from his jacket pocket. 'I stopped to watch your game. I haven't seen a cricket match for years, though I used to play here myself when I was a kid. I enjoyed the game.'

'Nice of you to say so,' said Akela. 'I'll get the Cubs to pack up as soon as they've had their tea, all right?'

'There's no hurry.' The stranger looked uneasy. 'I . . . I came to measure up the ground so I could mark out the boundaries for a timberyard. I'm . . .

I'm in the timber business. Fairclough, you've probably heard of me.'

Akela winced. 'It's a pity to spoil such a lovely site
with a timberyard,' he said, 'not that I object to
timberyards, or what you do with your land.'

'Aye, aye. I was just thinking the same. Seeing
your lads playing here made me realize there's more to
life than business. I could use the land by the disused
railway, though it would cost me more money to
clear it.'

Akela finished his sandwich. 'We'll be going now.
O.K., Cubs, tidy up now.'

''Ere, do you intend to come 'ere again?'

'We'd like to occasionally, if you wouldn't object.'

'That's all right by me. I'm not one to stop people
enjoying themselves. Take your time. You don't
have to leave in a hurry.'

'Thanks,' said Akela.

The stranger nodded and walked away, but had only
gone about ten metres, when he turned and came back.

'I think I'll develop that railway site after all,' he
said. 'I think I'll leave this land to the local council on
condition that it is never spoilt by future develop-
ment. Then you can play here as much as you like.'

'That's very kind of you,' said Akela.

'Aye,' said Fairclough. 'Aye. It's a pity to spoil this
place, as you say.'

The stranger nodded again and walked off. The Cubs watched him go.

'We've saved this land for posterity,' said Akela, somewhat surprised. 'Isn't that marvellous? We've saved a bit of old England.'

'Aye,' said Nobby. 'It's surprising what you can get for a jam sandwich.'

'Jam sandwich?' said Akela. 'He wouldn't give this land away for a jam sandwich. Toby Fairclough is the meanest man this side of the Pennines, that's why he's a millionaire. The reason Toby Fairclough left this land to the community, Nobby, is not because of a jam sandwich, but because he was impressed by the sportsmanship of the whole Pack.'

Nobby shrugged his shoulders.

'What you say might be true, I won't argue with you there, but on our next Pack outing, I think we ought to take twice as many jam sandwiches, just in case.'

'Just in case of what?' growled Akela, suspiciously.

'Just in case we get hungry,' said Nobby.

7 · Full bloom

THE Cubs gathered on the grassy hillside of West Park. The recent spate of Pack outings, all blessed with the finest weather, had made even the weediest Cub radiate health. They were bursting with energy, quick and alert, their gay hearts ready to drive their agile bodies to the challenge of a new game. They listened eagerly to Akela, for they knew he was about to reveal his evening's programme to them. Akela always planned his Pack outings to the finest detail, and that was one reason why he was regarded by his Cubs as the best Cub Scout Leader in Cheshire.

Akela inspected his Cubs, pretending he was not completely satisfied with their turn-out, but his suppressed smile told them, more than words themselves, that he was as proud of his Cubs as they were of him.

'I told you to polish your shoes, not your shoes and socks,' he growled at Nobby.

'I used a big brush,' answered Nobby, innocently.

'Looks to me as if you used a yard brush.' Akela

shook his head in mock desperation. 'How you can polish your shoes on those itchy, flat feet amazes me,' he said. 'Still, you tried, and that's worth nine points out of ten. Anyway, this evening we shall . . . let me see. Does anyone know how to play Scat?'

The Cubs shook their heads.

'I can play Snap,' said Nobby. 'See, you need two players . . .'

'You'll be playing it by yourself, if you don't watch out,' said Akela. 'As I was about to say, Scat is an ideal park game, for you need plenty of room to play it. It is a game which is known by many other names, but in this part of the country, we call it Scat. It is played between two equal sides, one team being the defenders, and the other team, the marauders. Now, the only equipment needed is three markers . . .'

Akela took a cap off each of three Cubs, and placed them on the ground to form a triangle, where each cap was about two metres from the other caps.

'This triangle is the defenders' castle, and the object of the game is for the defenders to capture the marauders and lock them up in this castle. So when I give the word to start, the marauders have to run off anywhere within the park grounds. Notice I say within the park grounds. On no account must anyone go outside the park grounds unless he has my permission, understand?'

The Cubs nodded, for they knew how strict Akela was with the Cubs in his charge.

'So the marauders run off and hide themselves where they can. The defenders count up to a hundred, to give the marauders a decent start, then they give chase. A marauder is caught when he is touched by a defender, then the defender brings him back and puts him in this castle. The defenders can leave one guard guarding the castle.

'The captured marauders must remain in the castle,' went on Akela, 'until a free marauder runs through the castle and shouts "Scat". Then the captured marauders may escape and have to be recaptured again. The game is won by the defenders when all the marauders have been captured. Any questions?'.

There were no questions. The Cubs were anxious to get on with the game.

'Good! Whilst you are playing the game, I shall sit on this park bench, behind the castle, watching you. I've got some reading to do for my exams next week. I shall not interfere with the game, but if I see any signs of objectionable un-Cub like behaviour, I shall have a word to say to the offender. Now marauders, get ready to run off. The game starts when I blow my whistle.'

The Cubs picked their sides. Akela put the whistle

to his lips and blew, and the marauding Cubs dashed away in all directions.

Snowy and Nobby ran down the hill, across the stone bridge and up the other hill to go behind the old manor house. Snowy knew the park well and already he had a plan in his mind. He came round the old manor house into a small secluded flower garden. The garden was screened on three sides by privet hedging, and on the fourth side by a clump of dense rhododendrons. Snowy nipped through a gap in the rhododendrons into an eerie interior provided by a dome of foliage, supported by a mass of tangled, twisted branches.

'They'll never find us here, Nobby,' said Snowy, 'and we can keep an eye on them without being seen.'

Snowy and Nobby crept across to the other side of the rhododendron clump. When they peered out, they could see clearly across the little valley to the castle on the opposite hillside. The defenders had gone off in pursuit of the marauders, and already three were returning with three captured marauders. Behind the castle, on the park bench, sat Akela, reading a book.

'I thought we could hide here until they've caught some of our side,' said Snowy, breathlessly, 'then we could make a break for the castle to release them.'

'Good idea, Snowy,' said Nobby. 'They've got three . . . four . . . five of us already. We'll wait until they've caught everyone but us, then we'll charge through the castle and release the lot.'

Nobby lay flat on the ground, well screened by the low foliage. He kept a sharp look-out. He put his hands to his eyes, pretending he was looking through binoculars.

'I'll . . . I'll go to the other side of the hideout,' said Snowy, 'in case any of the defenders creep behind us. If you hear me shout, you'll have to make a break for it alone, O.K.?'

'O.K., Snowy. I'll do the same for you from this side.'

'Don't make any noise. The defenders will have their ears open as well as their eyes.'

Snowy crept back over the crackling twigs to the other side of the rhododendron clump. He found himself a comfortable, well-covered position, from where he could keep an eye on the secluded garden. He could not see any defenders, but a teenage youth and his girlfriend walked around the gardens, arm in arm. They strode right up to the park bench, not more than a metre away from Snowy, quite unaware that anyone could see them. The youth put his arm around his girlfriend's shoulder and kissed her cheek.

Snowy was pleased Nobby wasn't with him to witness these young lovers, for Nobby would surely have made some caustic remark.

'Stop it, Billy,' said the girl, pushing away her boyfriend.

'Silly Billy!' Nobby probably would have said.

The girl looked at the circle of blooms set in the neat rectangular lawn, and in particular at a white orchid in full bloom. There were other orchids in this little sun-trap, but none as perfect as the one facing them.

'Isn't that orchid beautiful?' said the girl.

'What orchid?' said the boy.

'That white thing facing you. Can't you recognize an orchid yet?'

'Would you like it?'

'What do you mean?'

'If you want it, my chick, I'll get it for you.'

'You can't take that! You're not supposed to touch the park plants.'

'Nobody will know.'

'But you'll spoil the whole show if you take it away.'

'We won't be here to see it.'

'You are awful, Billy.'

Suddenly Snowy heard the hooting of an owl. It was Nobby.

'Whippet's been caught, Snowy,' said Nobby. 'Now they've caught nine of our side.'

Snowy crept across to Nobby. He peered through the foliage. True enough, there were nine marauders in the castle, but only one defender guarding them. The other defenders were combing the park for the remaining marauders.

'I think we'd better try rescuing the captured marauders now, before all the defenders come back,' said Snowy.

Nobby nodded.

'All right, Nobby,' continued Snowy. 'We'll attack the castle from two sides. You come in from the right, I'll come in from the left. There's only one guard – Bobbie. One of us is bound to get through.'

'O.K., Snowy.'

The two Cubs came out of their hideout and trotted down the hillside to the stream in the valley. They crossed the stone bridge and, still abreast, came up the hill to attack the castle. Bobbie came out to intercept them. Snowy moved to the left and Nobby to the right so Bobbie was forced to choose between them. He went after Snowy. Snowy made a detour round the back of the castle, allowing Nobby to come in unhindered from the other side.

'Snap!' said Nobby. 'Snap! Scat! Scat!'

The captured marauders scattered in all directions.

Everyone escaped, including Nobby who released them, but Snowy was captured and had to go inside the castle alone.

'We'll be back, Snowy,' said Nobby, waving to his pal.

Nobby turned and galloped down the hill, slapping his hip at the same time as if he was riding a galloping horse.

Snowy watched the marauders disappear in all sorts of cover, and sat in the middle of the castle. What worried him was not how quickly he could expect to be released, but whether or not the teenager would pull up the white orchid from the flower garden. Snowy wondered what he could do. So far, the youth had only talked of pulling up the orchid, but as yet he had committed no crime. Snowy pondered on his problem, and when he noticed a white paper-bag in a nearby litter basket, he suddenly had an idea.

'I'm just going to the litter basket,' he told Bobbie, the guard.

'You can't escape,' said Bobbie, firmly.

'I know,' said Snowy. 'I'm not going to try.'

Snowy got the paper-bag before Bobbie could stop him.

'May I borrow your pen, please?' Snowy asked Akela.

Akela gave Snowy his felt-tipped pen and carried on

reading his engineering textbook. Snowy returned to the castle and sat on the ground. Bobbie shrugged his shoulders and turned to watch out for approaching marauders.

Snowy smoothed out his paper-bag, and on one side, in bold letters, he wrote the words:

HANDS OFF BILLY

When he had finished, he folded up the bag and put it in his pocket, and returned the pen to Akela. Snowy then waited in the castle for his release.

But Snowy was not to be released. One by one, the other marauders were captured and put in the castle with Snowy. Nobby again made a valiant attempt to release them, but he was captured by Bobbie and put in with the other prisoners. Shortly afterwards, the last marauder was captured, and brought in triumph to the castle.

'Do we change sides now?' Nobby asked Akela.

Akela closed his textbook and looked at his watch. 'Not tonight, Nobby. We just have time to go back to the Cub headquarters for Flagdown.

So the Cubs walked back through the park. Snowy broke away unseen from the crowd, to make a short detour. He nipped through the rhododendron clump, keeping his eyes skinned for a forked stick. He found what he wanted, and when he reached the secluded garden he saw no one in sight. He put his forked stick through the paper-bag notice, and planted it beside the white orchid. Then he doubled back to catch up with the rest of the Cubs.

He found the Cubs in the car-park, where he saw Akela giving an old gentleman a hand to change a wheel. There was nothing Snowy could do to help, so he stood aside to watch.

Snowy's attention was then caught by the appearance of the teenage youth and his girlfriend. They ambled up to their motorcycle, and the youth took out a crash helmet from his pannier.

'I'll be back in a minute,' he said.

'Where are you going, Billy? said the girl.

'Never mind.'

'Don't you dare. Someone will see you.'

The youth draped his scarf over his crash helmet.

'I'll have it in the pannier before anyone knows.'

'Don't, Billy, don't.

But the youth had gone off in the direction of the secluded garden. The girl looked around anxiously, then casually pretended to check her make-up in the motorcycle mirror. She was a pretty girl, and Snowy realized she knew it by the way she admired herself in the mirror.

Within a minute, the youth returned, very red-faced.

'What have you been up to?' she asked.

'Nothing,' said the youth bashfully. 'I think you are right. The garden would be spoilt without that orchid.'

'I should think so, too,' said the girl, sharply. 'You should have more sense than to think about taking it. If you had, I wouldn't have spoken to you again. I don't want to be married to a jailbird.'

The couple put on their crash helmets and roared out of the car-park on their motorcycle. Akela replaced the hub cap on the wheel of the old gentleman's car and waved him on his way.

'Now we can go back to headquarters,' he said, 'I hope you've enjoyed your evening out.'

'Yes,' said Nobby. 'Scat's a good game.'

Akela nodded. 'It is nice to play a good game occasionally, especially at this time of year, in such beautiful surroundings as this park, but I don't suppose you noticed the beautiful surroundings.'

Nobby looked at Akela blankly. However Snowy had noticed the beautiful surroundings, and he hoped he had done something to keep them that way.

8 · Teabags

IT was another fine day, but it looked as though the wind might spring up at last, so Snowy decided to take his kite along to the Friday Cub meeting to give it a try out.

'Hi, Snow,' said Nobby, when Snowy called for him. 'You've . . . you've got your kite.'

'Yes, Nob,' said Snowy. 'I thought I might get it airborne tonight.'

It is strange, but everyone has a nickname at one time or another. It was understandable that the Cubs should call each other by their nicknames, but it was certainly surprising that Akela, of all people, should get himself a nickname – one which was to stick with him for a whole month. He was to be called 'Teabags'.

It all started when Snowy brought his kite along to that Friday-night Cub meeting. Snowy had built it months ago, during the winter, as part of a handcraft exercise. It was a good kite. It was a metre long, taller than Snowy himself, and almost as wide. It had a bamboo frame, covered with doped fabric, a

tail three metres long, and a tow-line three times the
length of a cricket pitch. The Cubs already assembled
on the back lawn behind their Cub headquarters when
Snowy and Nobby arrived, crowded round to see the
kite.

'Give us a demonstration, Snowy,' said Spotty,
elbowing his way to the front of the Cubs.

'If Akela doesn't mind,' said Snowy.

Akela came out on to the back lawn.

'Now then, what are you lot doing huddled up like a
rugby scrum?' he said. 'Ah, you've brought your kite
again, eh, Snowy?'

'The wind was up so I thought it would be a good
opportunity to give it a flight, if you don't mind.'

'Good idea, good idea. Yes, give us a demonstration,
Snowy, said Akela. 'Right, everybody stand back.
Snowy's going to give us a demonstration of kite-
flying.'

The Cubs stood back in the clearing behind the Cub
building. Akela looked about anxiously.

'Have you enough room, Snowy?' said Akela.
'There are some tall trees about.'

'Oh, there's plenty of room for me. It will be all
right once the kite's airborne,' said Snowy.

'Try it then. If you find you haven't enough room,
we can take it to West Park.'

'All right, I'll try it, but I won't promise anything

spectacular,' said Snowy. 'The wind is not as strong as I'd like it to be, but it's the best we've had for weeks.'

'Can I help, can I help?' said Nobby, enthusiastically, feeling the kite with his itchy fingers.

'You can hold the ball of string,' said Snowy.

'Good-o!' said Nobby, snatching the ball of string.

'Steady, steady,' cautioned Akela, 'you're not competing in an all-in wrestling match.' But he let the Cubs sort themselves out.

'Stand in the corner, Nobby, and pay out the line as I take the kite away,' said Snowy. His instructions were firm and clear.

Nobby stood right in the corner of the clearing. Snowy, holding the kite right up so it would not scrape the ground, slowly backed away right across the clearing to drag out the tow-line.

'Hold the line fairly taut,' shouted Snowy. 'I'll wait for a gust of wind.'

Snowy held up his kite in the launching position, and when he felt the wind tug at the fabric, he let his kite go. The kite soared up like a lift. Snowy ran across the clearing to Nobby.

'Pay out the line, Nobby,' he called.

But Nobby, not having the feel of kite-flying, held on to the line as tight as he could. Snowy gently took it from him.

'I've got it now, Nobby,' he said calmly.

Snowy paid out the line steadily. The kite rose higher and higher in the wind, until there was no more line to pay out. Akela nodded in approval.

'Not bad,' he said. 'Umm, not bad at all.'

Snowy could do no more than hold on to the end of the line. He felt the steady pull, and watched the kite sway from side to side against the blue sky.

'Anyone else want to hold it?' he said, holding out the wooden spool to which was attached the end of the tow-line.

'Ooh, yeah,' said Nobby, enviously.

Nobby reached out for the spool, tripped over Whippet who was trying to see better, and fell flat on his face. The tow-line went slack and caught the top of a sycamore tree. Nobby, still on the ground, snatched up the spool and gave the tow-line a good tug to free it from the top branches. The tow-line broke, and the kite nose-dived on the other side of the trees. Akela clenched his fits.

'Oh, sorry, Snow,' said Nobby. 'I'll get it for you.'

Before Akela could stop him, Nobby dashed off like a little bunny. He squeezed through a beech hedge surrounding the Cub Scout grounds, jumped across a stream, and scurried down the footpath after the kite. The 2nd Billington Cub Scout Pack went after him like a pack of bloodhounds.

'Take it easy, take it easy,' shouted Akela, going after them via the Cub ground entrance, at a more civilized pace, to make sure they came to no harm.

The wind somersaulted the kite across an open field. Nobby caught up with it, but as it did not stay still for long enough for him to pick it up, he jumped on it. When Akela and Snowy caught up, they found Nobby holding up the shapeless kite, its frame broken in two places.

'You clumsy thing,' said Akela. 'Why did you have to jump on it?'

'I . . . I stopped it from blowing away,' said Nobby, innocently.

'You did that right enough.'

Snowy picked up his broken kite.

'Sorry, Snowy,' said Nobby. 'If I had some money, I'd buy you another one, but I'm a bit short this month.'

Snowy pouted, then said, 'Don't worry, Nobby. I can mend it.'

'It would be far easier to build a new kite if you ask me,' growled Akela, angrily. Suddenly he had an idea. 'Listen, lads,' he said, waving his Cubs around him. 'Snowy had a good kite until this little elephant jumped on it. What I propose is that we should all build him another. I can get the materials. We've plenty of money in the Cub funds. Everybody can do a little bit to help, and it will be a grand exercise. When we've built it, we can have a Pack outing to some quiet spot to give it a test flight. Snowy can have it when we've finished with it. How about that?'

The Cubs cheered. A Pack outing with Akela was a delight at any time, and the thought of doing handcraft at their next few meetings, caught all their imaginations.

'We are not going to build any rubbish, you know,' said Akela. 'I want this to be the best kite that's ever been built in the whole county. Two Cubs, Spotty and Louie, get the blackboard from the hall. Podge, you bring out the easel. Whippet, you get the rubber and chalks. Bring them outside on to the lawn. I'll show you what I've in mind.'

The Cubs jostled back to the Cub headquarters. When they had assembled the blackboard on the back lawn, Akela revealed his plans. On the blackboard, he drew the shape of a kite.

'I'd like to make it fairly large,' he said, 'so you can all have a reasonably sized bit to work on, since making it is going to be a Pack effort.'

Akela marked in the details. It was to be two metres long and one and a half metres wide.

'That . . . that will be a bit taller than you,' said Snowy.

'A bit,' mused Akela, 'but it should be no more difficult to build. In fact you'll find it easier to build than a flimsy paper job. Flimsy jobs won't last more than five minutes, especially if Nobby's around.'

Not only did Akela design the kite, but he also designed a drum for holding the tow-line. The tow-line was to be nearly 100 metres long. The drum was to be mounted in a sturdy frame, which had two spikes underneath to anchor it to the ground.

'If you do a job,' said Akela, 'I say you should do a job properly. I'll pick up the materials first thing tomorrow. If any of you would like to help, be here at ten o'clock in the morning. We'll need all the help we can get.'

The next day kept seventeen volunteers busy. Every Cub who could come along had something to do, measuring, sawing, sanding. gluing, cutting, stitching, doping, knotting, screwing, painting. The huge kite took shape on the back lawn. They doped it green and red, the Pack colours. They painted the drum assembly to match. By the end of the afternoon it was almost ready. Akela looked at his watch.

'All we have to do now is to wait for the paint to dry,' he said.

Akela went into the Cub headquarters to get his portable radio. The Cubs crowded round it when he switched it on, to listen to the weather forecast. Then Akela made his announcement.

'The weather forecast is just what we want,' he chuckled. 'Winds gusting to twenty knots. We'll leave the kite overnight in the hall to dry, then tomorrow we'll go to Blackpool to give it a test flight.'

The Cubs whooped with glee. This was the news they had been waiting for.

Blackpool sands were almost deserted that Sunday morning when they took down their equipment. There was a beachcomber, and a man exercising his dog. There were a couple of yachts out to sea, and a racing canoe, handled by what appeared to be an expert, in a yellow waterproof outfit. The wind

blew out from the land, which suited them perfectly,
for it would take the kite over the roomy sea, away
from the tall inland obstructions. Everything in fact
seemed ideal, apart from the tide which was coming in,
but it is seldom possible to have everything.

Akela gave the Cubs their jobs. First they
anchored the tow-line drum in the sand. It was the
job of Podge, the heaviest Cub in the Pack, to sit on a
crossmember to keep it stable. Other Cubs paid out
the line, while others assembled the huge kite. The
kite stirred in the breeze, as if anxious to get airborne. The Cubs, well drilled, carried it almost to the
edge of the sea. There, they held it firmly, until the

tow-line was attached, then all was ready for Akela's final instructions.

'Standby, Cubs at the drum,' shouted Akela. 'Prepare to release the brake lever. Raise the kite above your heads . . .'

The wind across the open beach snatched the kite from the hands of the six Cubs who formed the launching party.

'Let the brake lever go,' shouted Akela. 'Steady! Not too fast . . .'

Once the brake lever released the ratchet, the kite drew the tow-line from the revolving drum. It soared up like a giant eagle.

'Hold it!' warned Akela. 'Let it out, steady . . . a little at a time.'

The tow-line, almost all of it, was steadily paid out. The kite pulled like an angry whale, but the tow-line and its anchorage were firm. Akela smiled. He clamped the brake lever on so the kite would not take the tow-line off the drum.

'If the launching party hadn't let go when they did, they would have been up there with it now.'

This was the result of their previous day's hard work and every Cub was proud of his efforts. They took it in turn to look at the hovering kite through Akela's binoculars. The kite was like a captive animal, constantly trying to break free. It was quite high, higher than the local church tower, and that had a hundred steps to the top.

Snowy was the last of the Cubs to use the binoculars After he had studied the performance of the kite, he trained his sights on the sea below. He focused the glasses on a canoe, and to his surprise, he saw there was no one in it. It looked as if it was upside down. He frowned, looked again, then he called Akela.

'That canoe,' he said, 'I think it's rolled over.'

Akela looked up. 'I think you're right, Snowy,' he gasped, 'Cubs, stay where you are!' Then kicking off his shoes and dropping his jacket, he ran off to the sea.

The situation must have been critical, for Akela plunged straight into the waves. He swam out towards the canoe. Snowy tried to keep him in focus with the binoculars. He saw Akela reach the canoe, and the canoe right itself. The canoeist, protected by his weatherproof garments, seemed none the worse for wear. Akela trod water, beside him, keeping watch. Snowy thought he was thinking of a way to get the canoe to the safety of the shore, and tried to think of a way to help them.

'If only we could get a line out to them,' said Snowy under his breath.

The only line they had was the kite tow-line, but that would do the trick if only it could be got out to Akela. The situation called for drastic action.

Snowy had the germ of an idea. He knocked off the brake lever on the tow-line drum. The kite pulled away and took the tow-line clean off the drum. Now, having nothing to hold it in a stable attitude, the kite cartwheeled and nose-dived. The tow-line lay down in the sea, not more than twenty metres from Akela and the canoeist.

Snowy shouted to Akela to grab the line, and at the same time he tried to pull the line in. Akela heard him apparently, for he swam towards the kite.

'Give a hand to haul in the line,' said Snowy to his Cub friends, pulling as hard as he could.

The other Cubs quickly joined in. When they had retrieved sufficient line, Snowy attached the end to the drum and used the crank handle to wind it in.

Somehow, or for some strange reason, Akela lifted the kite and it caught the wind. Immediately the kite tried to climb away, but with Akela hanging on to it, it flapped and twisted like an untied sail. To Snowy, it looked like a captured swan trying to break free.

The Cubs heaved on the line for all they were worth, but all their efforts did nothing to pacify the flapping kite, in fact they assisted in stabilizing it.

Suddenly the kite dragged Akela almost clean out of the water, so much so that all except his legs below the knees was clear of the surface. The wind

dropped and Akela was plunged back into the sea. Another gust of wind caught the kite and again it strained to get airborne. It seemed that whenever the Cubs gave a good heave on the line, or a gust of wind caught the fabric, the kite wanted to take off.

'Heave!' shrieked Nobby in desperation. 'Heave Heave! Heave!'

All this was too much for the kite. The fabric ripped open and was torn by the wind completely from its frame. Part of the frame dropped away too, but the main spar remained attached to the tow-line. Once again, Akela was dunked in the sea.

Now the Cubs could haul in Akela, who clung to the

main spar for all he was worth. The Cubs brought him ashore and assisted him out of the water.

'How is the canoeist?' asked Snowy, embarrassed that they had rescued the wrong man.

Akela coughed and spluttered. 'The canoeist was simply practising Eskimo rolls,' he spluttered. 'He's an international canoeing instructor. He said he didn't want to be rescued.'

Again Akela coughed.

'Have you caught a cold?' asked Nobby, sympathetically.

'What do you mean, have I caught a cold?'

Nobby shrugged his shoulders. 'I mean, well . . . are you all right, in the pink, as they say?'

Akela coughed. 'In the pink? Would you be in the pink if you were dunked in and out of the sea like a teabag on the end of a bit of string?'

Akela was not amused, but Nobby laughed. That set all the Cubs laughing. Akela took off his vest and shirt and squeezed the water out of them. Nobby rolled on the sand, helpless with laughter.

'Teabags . . .' he howled. 'Teabags . . . on the end of a bit . . . of string . . .'

That was how Akela got his nickname, and it stuck for a whole month. Another nickname was coined that day too. Mrs Clark could not for the life of her understand why Nobby should call her teabags 'akelas'.

9 · Maiden voyage

THE Cubs were up bright and early for their Pack outing to Lawton Quarry, bright like the weather, early because the weather forecast was not so promising, and the Cubs were anxious to enjoy the good weather whilst they could. A Pack outing to a disused quarry may not be regarded as an interesting day out, but the 2nd Billington Cubs were excited about it. Lawton Quarry was now a huge lake which had been developed as a recreational area. The countryside around the lake had not only been tidied up, but had been cultivated according to the best landscape designs. What had been a scar on the countryside, was now an area of outstanding scenic beauty.

'Teabags' had brought his Cubs to the area to show them, amongst other things, that the knots they learnt to tie at their Cub meetings were indeed used in practice.

Teabags parked the Scout mini-bus in the shade of

the lakeside spruce trees, and opened the rear doors to let the Cubs tumble out. Nobby goggled at the huge expanse of water.

'Wow, what a big billabong,' he gasped.

Why he should use the term 'billabong', which is an Australian aboriginal word for water-hole, no one knew, not that it mattered.

'As you say, Nobby,' said Teabags, 'it is a big billabong. Now, on the other side of this billabong is a building, which is used as a club hut by the Lawton Sailing Club. Later today, we shall see them in action, and I'd like you to notice the knots they use. Make a note of them in your notebooks, and at the end of the day we'll see who has spotted the most types of knots.'

The Cubs walked out on to a little wooden pier. They were early, for as yet there were no signs of any boating or sailing, and little activity in general, but they had not long to wait, for almost immediately a mini-van drew up beside them, on top of which was a small boat. The boat looked more like a punt than anything else. The owner untied the ropes which lashed the craft to the car-rack, and Snowy recorded in his notebook; round turn and four half hitches, granny knot and reef knot.

As soon as Teabags saw what the man was doing, he got his Cubs to give him a hand.

'It's quite light,' said the man, as they lowered the

craft to the ground. 'I designed it myself, you can see it's just plywood and doped canvas. The sides are solid plywood. The bottom is doped fabric stretched across a dozen horizontal cross members. I suppose you could describe it as a lightweight punt, but it has many advantages over the conventional type of craft. It is more manoeuvrable, faster, cheaper and easier to build, and you can carry it round on top of a car, or on top of your head for that matter.' The man laughed at his own joke, but nobody else laughed with him. 'All I want to do now,' went on the man, 'is to give it its water trials, then I'll be all set to put it on the market. In a couple of years, there'll be more of

these on the canals and rivers of Britain than any
other single type, you mark my words.'

Teabags shrugged his shoulders. 'Why don't you
test it on a canal or river. If that's what it's designed
for . . .'

'Ha, ha,' said the man, cunningly. 'I want space
enough to give it a good testing. I don't do things by
half measures. As I told you, this craft will be highly
manoeuvrable. I want to give it a good try-out before
I put it on the market. An invention is no good unless
it is thoroughly tried and tested.'

The Cubs helped to carry the lightweight punt
down the slipway and slid it into the water. Nobby
picked up a long pole from the grass.

'Are you a pole-vaulter, mister?' he said.

The inventor snatched the pole. 'That's to propel
the punt,' he said, then taking his pole with him, he
climbed over the back seat of the punt and walked
along its whole length until he was able to stand on
the flat, plywood bow. The bow dipped alarmingly,
but it did not go under. The inventor jabbed his pole
into the water at the side of the punt and pushed
hard. The punt moved away from the pier quite
quickly. The Cubs cheered. The craft was nippy.

The inventor acknowledged the applause and
jabbed his pole in a second time. He pushed hard and
increased his speed. The craft seemed to be going

quite well. The inventor then tried another push, but unfortunately the water was so deep that he almost failed to touch the bottom with his pole. The pole went down and down so that only about ten centimetres were clear of the water, and the inventor had to get down on his hands and knees to give the pole a good push.

'The lake's twenty metres deep in the middle!' warned Teabags.

The result of all this was that the inventor lost hold of his pole. The punt drifted away, and the ten centimetres of visible pole slowly leaned over and disappeared from view under the wind-ruffled surface.

'I've lost my pole,' called the inventor sheepishly.

The wind caught the lightweight punt and slowly took it out into deeper water. The inventor was in no immediate danger, but it was difficult to see how, without any means of propulsion, he could possibly return to the shore.

'Hold your shirt open and you'll sail to the other side,' shouted Nobby.

But it was a long way to the other side, and the inventor wasn't very keen to go.

'There's a rope in the back of my car,' shouted the inventor. 'Can you get it and pull me back?'

Teabags sent two of his Cubs, Bobbie and Podge, to get the rope, and he himself got a lifebelt from its stowage position on the pier. He tied one end of the inventor's rope to a post on the end of the pier, using a bowline, and the other end to the line already attached to the lifebelt, with a reef knot. Now he had a good thirty metres of rope attached to the lifebelt.

'Lie down in the bottom of your boat and I'll throw the lifebelt across,' said Teabags.

The inventor lay down in the bottom of his punt. Teabags threw out the lifebelt. It curled through the air, taking the line with it, and dropped in the water on the far side of the punt. The inventor sat up, clutched the line draped across the punt and pulled in the lifebelt.

'I've got it! Thanks.'

'We'll soon pull you ashore now,' said Teabags.

Teabags got his Cubs to heave on the line to pull in the punt. All went well, and the punt was steadily drawn in towards the shore.

At this time, a little dinghy with an outboard motor chugged across the lake, with its helmsman in the uniform of the commodore of the sailing club. He dropped newly-painted marker buoys in position, ready for the afternoon's sailing races. He came to pass the punt, although he kept well clear so as to cause no anxiety. The punt was no more than spitting distance from the pier, and the motor dinghy was a good twenty metres away.

Suddenly the motor dinghy flipped over on its back, throwing the commodore into the water. The motor stopped, the dinghy nose-dived so that the outboard motor was raised clear of the water. The broken punting pole and a couple of marker buoys drifted to the surface to complete the scene.

Teabags slipped the rope off the pier post and dropped it in the water.

'Throw him the lifebelt,' he shouted to the inventor in the punt. 'Quickly! He may need help.'

The inventor threw the lifebelt to the commodore, now in the water, and pulled his punt over to rescue

him. Somehow the line became entangled with the
wrecked dinghy, but all was sorted out. The commodore was not hurt, and he was soon pulled into the
punt. Yet the danger was not yet over. Although the
helpless punt was no more than fifteen metres from
the end of the little pier, it was in deep water, and
Snowy realized he was watching a real-life drama.

But Teabags was quite calm in the circumstances.

'Throw me the line and I'll pull both of you in
together,' he said.

The inventor threw Akela the line and the Cubs
pulled them in without further mishap. Teabags
moored the punt to the pier, the two men were then
helped ashore, and the wrecked dinghy was dragged
up the slipway. The dinghy had a split along the
whole length of the underside of its hull. The commodore was not amused.

'I was putting out the marker buoys for this
afternoon's race,' he moaned. 'How do you think I
can mark out the course now?'

'You must have hit my punt pole,' said the
inventor.

'Punt pole?' said the commodore. 'Why did you
leave a punt pole in the water? What are you trying
to do, kill somebody?'

'I'm sorry,' said the inventor. 'I didn't mean to . . .
I was only testing out my new invention.' Suddenly

the inventor snapped his fingers. 'Why not use my punt to put out your marker buoys? You can clamp your outboard motor on the back of the rear seat. I designed my boat for adaptability as well as high speeds and manoeuvrability. See these plywood sides? They extend below the hull to form two parallel keels to give it stability. The canvas hull is light, and when it moves, the air gets between the hull and the surface of the water, lifts it up and reduces drag. At about ten knots, the hull will be completely clear of the water, like a hovercraft, but the keels, and this is the clever bit, will still be in the water, giving the craft stability.'

'What, that old box?' said the commodore. 'I've . . . I've been sailing for nearly forty years now, and I've never seen anything so ridiculous in all my life.'

'Why not?' said the inventor. 'People used to laugh at the Wright brothers' early biplanes, but they were soon laughing on the other side of their faces. I tell you, my boat's a world-beater. Let me borrow your outboard motor and I'll prove it to you.'

The commodore reluctantly unclamped his outboard motor from his wreck. 'I must be as crazy as you are,' he said. 'Well, at least you can drive me across to the club house.'

'Let me give you a demonstration first. You're a sailing man. You'll soon appreciate what I mean.'

So the two men fixed the outboard motor to the back of the punt, started it up and moved off. Unfortunately the punt was still moored to the pier. As the mooring-rope tightened, it caught the back of Nobby's leg.

'Yeowh!' yelled Nobby. He overbalanced, then realizing he was going to fall off the pier and nothing in the world could save him, he put his hands together, as if he was saying a little prayer, and dived into the water.

'Man overboard!' shouted Snowy.

When Nobby surfaced, he was close enough to the pier to grab one of the supporting posts and Snowy was near enough to pull him out. Teabags uncoiled the mooring-rope from the end post and threw it into the bottom of the punt.

'Don't worry about the little fellow,' said Teabags, pointing to Nobby. 'We'll soon dry him out.'

So the punt went out once again. Teabags took Nobby back to the Scout mini-bus. There Nobby was given a towel and a blanket to wrap himself in. Teabags had come prepared for any emergency. As for the punt, it bounced across the lake in grand style. It seemed to live up to every expectation of its inventor, then suddenly it stopped in the middle of the lake and began to sink. Apparently the pounding had split the canvas floor. However, there were now a few sailing dinghies in the area, and they all swarmed in to give assistance.

'You aren't the only one to have a dip in the billabong,' said Teabags.

Nobby shivered in his blanket. 'Well, that's the last dip I ever want to have. It's worse than washing! That billabong is freezing.'

Teabags looked up at the sky. Dark clouds had already scudded across the sun, and the wind had freshened.

'It looks as if the weather is about to break at last,' said Teabags. 'Never mind, we've made the most of the fine weather whilst we could. Next week we'll be back in the Cub headquarters, catching up on all our indoor activities. I expect you are looking forward to telling us the Cub Scout Promise and Law, Nobby.'

'But ... but ... but ... but ... but ...,' said Nobby.

'You sound like a little motorboat,' said Teabags. 'Never mind but ... but ... but ... You know your Promise and Law well enough. Tell me ...'

'A Cub Scout promises to look his best,' began Nobby hopefully. 'He thinks ... thinks ... sinks ... stinks ...' Nobby groaned and walked away.

'Where's he going?' said Teabags, in alarm.

Snowy looked up. 'I ... I think he's going to jump back in the billabong!' he yelled.

On the following pages you will find some other exciting Beaver Books to look out for in your local bookshop

EMIL AND HIS CLEVER PIG

Astrid Lindgren

Emil, the naughty little Swedish boy, is up to mischief again!
First he paints his sister blue, then he sets fire to the parson's
wife, and then he locks his father in the lavatory! And on
Tuesday the tenth of August, he does something so bad that
his mother won't even write about it in the blue exercise book
(but *you* read about it here).

THE CUCUMBER KING

Christine Nostlinger

It is Easter Sunday morning when the Hogelmann family find the Cucumber King sitting on their kitchen table. Wearing a golden crown, white cotton gloves and red varnish on his toenails, King Kumi-Ori the Two has been evicted from his kingdom by his subjects' *coup d'etat,* and throws himself on the mercy of the Hogelmanns. With his overbearing manner and sly habits he quickly makes himself unpopular – except with Dad, whose reactionary instincts are roused by the royal presence. Meanwhile young Wolfie and his sister Martina make friends with the King's oppressed ex-subjects – and the scene is set for conflict.

Set in Austria, this highly original and very funny story will enthral all who read it.

AGATON SAX AND THE CRIMINAL DOUBLES

Nils-Olof Franzén

The small town of Bykoping in Sweden is famous for only one thing — it is the home of Agaton Sax. Being a world-famous master detective makes him a target for the criminal underworld, and two dastardly gangleaders, Octopus Scott and Julius Mosca, fly in to deal with him. But their arrival coincides with that of the unfortunate Charlie MacSnuff and Absalom Nick, who keep being arrested as they are the doubles of Scott and Mosca. The ensuing muddle defeats everyone — or almost everyone!

A wonderful blend of humour and excitement for readers of eight and over.

URSULA BEAR

Sheila Lavelle

Ursula likes bears – big bears, little bears, fat bears, thin bears, in fact, any kind of bears. So when she finds a magic spell to turn a little girl into a bear, she is thrilled to bits!

And when the circus comes to town, and she can't afford a ticket, turning herself into a bear seems to be a very good idea. The trouble is, things are never quite as simple as they seem . . .

If you're an eager Beaver reader, perhaps you ought to try some more of our exciting titles. They are available in bookshops or they can be ordered directly from us. Just complete the form below and enclose the right amount of money and the books will be sent to you.

☐	HELLO MR. TWIDDLE	Enid Blyton	80p
☐	THE ENCHANTED WOOD	Enid Blyton	95p
☐	THE MAGIC FARAWAY TREE	Enid Blyton	95p
☐	HEIDI'S SONG		95p
☐	BILLY BOOT'S BRAINWAVE	Elizabeth Gard	95p
☐	URSULA BEAR	Sheila Lavelle	75p
☐	NICHOLAS ON HOLIDAY	Goscinny and Sempé	90p
☐	EMIL IN THE SOUP TUREEN	Astrid Lindgren	85p
☐	REBECCA'S WORLD	Terry Nation	90p
☐	THE TERRIBLY PLAIN PRINCESS	Pamela Oldfield	95p
☐	LOLLIPOP	Christine Nostlinger	£1.00
☐	THE WORST KINDS IN THE WORLD	Barbara Robinson	75p
☐	THE BROWNIES IN HOSPITAL	Pamela Sykes	95p
☐	THE GREAT ICE CREAM CRIME	Hazel Townson	85p
☐	THE MILL HOUSE CAT	Marjorie Ann Watts	£1.00
☐	BOGWOPPIT	Ursula Moray Williams	95p

And if you would like to hear more about Beaver Books, and find out all the latest news, don't forget the Beaver Bulletin. If you just send a stamped, self-addressed envelope to Beaver Books, 17-21 Conway Street, London W1P 6JD and we will send you one.

If you would like to order books, please send this form with the money due to:

HAMLYN PAPERBACK CASH SALES, PO BOX 11, FALMOUTH, CORNWALL TR10 9EN.

Send a cheque or postal order, and don't forget to include postage at the following rates: UK: 55p for the first book, 22p for the second, 14p for each additional book; BFPO and Eire: 55p for the first book, 22p for the second, 14p for the next seven books and 8p per book thereafter. Overseas: £1.00 for first book and 25p for each additional book.

NAME...

ADDRESS..

....

Please print clearly